A WAY OF
HIS OWN

A WAY OF HIS OWN

T.A. Dyer

Houghton Mifflin Company   Boston

1981

Library of Congress Cataloging in Publication Data
Dyer, Thomas A
    A way of his own.
    SUMMARY: A lame boy from a very primitive
nomadic tribe is abandoned by his family and, together with a girl stolen from another tribe,
tries to survive a cruel winter.
    [1. Survival — Fiction.   2. Physically handi-
capped — Fiction]   I. Title.
PZ7.D9885Wey   [Fic]   81–350
ISBN 0–395–30443–1   AACR1

Printed in the United States of America.

P 10 9 8 7 6 5 4 3 2 1

To Paul and Lila Morter

"COME ON." Yaiya and Shutok were both on their hands and knees. The bison, a lone bull, had spotted them but it had not been alarmed at their approach.

"Come on," he said again. It was the same way he talked to his burden bundle whenever he could not get it to tie up right. Yaiya was impatient with everything and everyone, even himself.

"Isn't this close enough?" Shutok whispered.

"For spear-throwers, perhaps. Not spears."

"I know that." Shutok understood this part of the hunt well. He had seen it often, and he and Yaiya had practiced it as long as he could remember. But there were important parts of the hunt he did not understand — parts kept secret by the hunters — and Shutok was just as heedful of the way as he was wary of the huge bull.

"This is not a rabbit," he said. "What is it you hope to do by getting closer?"

"Kill it. What else could you think?"

"Yaiya, this is evil and you know it. Only hunters can kill bison."

"Come on. And stop talking or you will spook it. Or are you afraid?" he grinned.

"No," Shutok lied. "I am not afraid." But even the hunters avoided outcast bulls. The herds drove the short-tempered, old animals away because they were dangerous, unpredictably so.

Instead, the hunters lured bison from the herds. They crawled through the prairie grass the same way that Shutok and Yaiya were crawling now, except hunters wore wolf pelts and carried throwers for their tipped spears. When they were close enough for the herd animals to see them, the men slowly waved their wolf tails in the air. One or two of the curious bison would leave the herd to approach the hunters. When an animal was close enough the hunters attacked. It was only by adopting the teamwork of a wolf pack that the hunters were able to keep an animal so harried and confused that it did not charge one of them.

But an outcast bull might attack hunters — it might do anything.

Shutok followed his brother. He did not feel like a wolf in a pack; in front of him the renegade towered taller than the tallest man, and he was a boy with a pointed stick for a spear. When they were very close to the bull Yaiya waved his stick back and forth to attract it even closer. It watched the motion, its eyes indifferent and dull, but when it made a low belching sound both of the boys understood the warning. They were so close to the beast that they heard the flies swarm and settle again when it twitched its flanks.

"We are too close to the bull. It could charge."

"Shut up!" Yaiya snarled. He waved his stick.

"What! Ho, you boys there!" It was Mato, whooping and making a racket behind them.

"Watch out!" Shutok called to Yaiya. He rolled away and the bull like a boulder thundering down a mountainside made the ground and the air quake, its split hooves coming so close to Shutok that he felt the shaggy fur brush against his skin.

"Oh," he groaned. He had wrenched his back again. The boy lay looking up at the bison. The enormous animal loomed over him like a great cloud, pawing at the ground and thrashing its horns through the grass before charging at him.

"Go away," Shutok begged helplessly. When the bull raised its tail straight up and bellowed, the boy closed his eyes. Once more he heard the hooves, but going away this time, and when he opened his eyes Yaiya was standing over him.

Yaiya looked scared. "Where did it hit you?" he asked, his hands trembling as he reached down to help his brother.

"Ouch! Don't do that. It didn't hit me."

"Well, get up. Mato saw the whole thing and she will tell Ala for sure. We are really in trouble now. We can't let Ala think you are hurt. Get up."

"I will be all right," he said, but first he had to contain the burning in his legs and spine. Like building a ring around a fire, letting his backbone settle was a deliberate fitting into place of scattered, uneven stones. Shutok felt best lying flat on his back with his knees pulled up. Sometimes this was the only way he could find relief from the pain and the strength to stand.

"Here comes Ala," Yaiya fretted. Shutok sat up, pushing himself off the ground with his arms.

The sky was overcast and dull but their mother looked as if she were walking directly into the sun. There were wrinkles at the corners of her eyes and between her eyebrows. It was not a squint. It was worry. "You have broken the way," she said to them.

"We weren't doing anything."

"Perhaps not. But you must not be too anxious to become hunters. The hunters guard the way, and you will be judged ready when you show respect for the laws. Breaking them will only bring evil upon us all."

"But I am ready," Yaiya swelled. "I only break the laws because Aar won't send me after power when he can clearly see that I am ready. I could have killed that old bull with just this wooden spear if Mato had not made it run."

"Yaiya," she said, sitting, "you do not listen. What must happen? Does the sky have to split open or the earth boil forth before you will respect the way? These things and worse could happen if you offend the Master of the Animals with your pride. Let me tell you again. The hunters have many secrets, but this much I know.

"It was when all the people were animals," she began. "Like the bison and the deer, the people ate no meat, but roots and berries instead. It was then that a shaman came among them in the form of a wolf and he said, 'I will find the food to make you strong.'

4

"So the shaman began on a long journey all alone out onto the prairie. There was no food there and still he went on alone. He was near death from starvation before he happened to overtake a bison.

" 'Brother bison,' said the shaman who was a wolf, 'Is there no food here that you can share with me?'

" 'I will give you food to make you strong,' answered the bison. Now the shaman knew it was really the Master of the Animals speaking to him with the bison's voice, for there was no food and he could plainly see that. As far as the earth stretched out before his eyes there was only the prairie grass, and the wolf asked what he must do in order to eat.

" 'You must prove the power of your medicine. First you must kill me,' said the Master of the Animals with the bison's voice.

"The shaman was puzzled by this, for was this bison not his brother? He said nothing, did nothing, only listened.

" 'And if you succeed in killing me,' the Master of the Animals continued, 'Then you must follow the way, or the meat will give you no strength. You must treat all your brothers with respect. Do not insult their spirits by killing when you are not worthy. Do not kill without need. Do not waste.

" 'Do this and there will always be meat to give you strength. But abandon the way, and your brothers will abandon you. Evil will attack you. Starvation. Sickness. Weakness and death!'

"The wolf who was a shaman quickly killed the bison

then. The Master of the Animals watched to see what the shaman did. He cut up the meat without letting any of it touch the ground, even as our hunters do by placing the meat on the skin of the beast. The Master of the Animals saw that this was honorable.

"Before eating any of the meat himself, the shaman carried what he had taken from the bison back to the people who were animals. And the people wasted nothing. The Master of the Animals saw that this was honorable also.

"The shaman was the first hunter, and he ate his share of the meat away from the women. This became the way, and much more, too. It is much better to die than to be unworthy of one's deeds. This is what I want you to remember. For breaking the way is an insult to the Master of the Animals and it threatens all your people with great evil."

"But Mato chased it away," Yaiya said. "There was no harm done."

"No. There was no harm done. Come walk with me back to camp."

As they stood, Shutok noticed how Yaiya glanced back at the old bison. The bull was grazing its way toward them again, and the expression on his brother's face said, "I'll get you next time." He threw his spear ahead of himself, then ran to get it.

"It is the evil again, isn't it?" Ala asked as soon as Yaiya was gone. "The same evil of the winter. I can tell by the way you are walking."

"It is nothing," the boy assured her.

"You should be weak after such a winter, Shutok. It was a hungry time. But there has been enough time now for your strength to return. The others have noticed. When you run, you limp, and you have trouble keeping up with the rest of us."

"Mato made the bison charge us, that is all. I hurt myself getting away from it, but I will be better by morning," he promised.

"Perhaps, but I think it is more than that. It is an evil one. The others blame you for breaking the way and bringing it upon yourself. With Mato pregnant, it worries them. What if this evil crawls out of you at night when we are all sleeping together around the fire? Will it go into the rest of us as well? It is not good the way everyone watches you. If anything goes wrong they will blame you for it."

They walked a while without talking. Their camp came into sight, nothing more than a bald spot on the prairie with a small, smoky fire burning in the center of it. There were no shelters, no wooden racks for drying meat. Having eaten their dogs during the hard winter, the survivors in Shutok's band — eight of them — were following the herds this season with only what they themselves could carry. Beyond the camp was the waterhole and the carcass of the bison that the hunters had killed the day before, a dust devil of buzzards wheeling over it. Farther yet, the herds spread over the prairie as far as the horizon, broad rivers of animals changing course and shape as they drifted across the landscape.

"Look," Shutok muttered. Ahead of them, Yaiya had

stopped to watch the hunters rework the stone points they had used in yesterday's hunt. "They let him stand there, but if I go close to them they drive me away."

"You know that is the way. The hunters always stay apart from women and children, for fear that they will lose their strength."

"Then why does Yaiya get to watch them?" he insisted.

"Because he is older than you."

"One year only."

"Yes, but soon he will be sent after power. Sooner, maybe, than is fitting. With only three of them to hunt, they need his help."

The sound of chipping stopped when Ala and Shutok approached the circle of men. The boy felt their eyes looking him over critically for the catch in his step. He could not conceal it. He wanted to walk past them, but when Aar spoke to his mother, he had to stand obediently and listen.

"We go to the river tomorrow," the man said.

"Do you hear, Shutok? We will be moving on after making a kill just yesterday. It does not give us much time to rest." Ala spoke loudly to the boy. The weak words of women and children could be safely overheard by the hunters, but only a hunter could speak directly to another. That was the way.

"I do not need to rest," Shutok boasted thinly.

"But I wonder why so soon." Ala sometimes came dangerously close to questioning the decisions of the hunters. The boy's body was full of tension and he wanted to go lie down with his knees pulled up.

"We do not have enough stone for hunting," Aar said. "It is far to go, but we need to make points from the shiny black rocks that can be found there." Shutok looked at the ground but he felt the man's eyes on him when he added, "We will run."

"Then we must eat our fill today, Shutok. Come along with us, Yaiya."

"But I want to stay with . . ."

"Go!" Aar ordered.

Yaiya glared at his brother. "I do not need to rest, either," he said. Yaiya did not like to be reminded that he was a boy, and Shutok was the only one for him to be angry with. "And we will see who can run. I dare you to keep up with me tomorrow."

THEY RAN ALL afternoon, trying to make the river by nightfall, but they put their burdens down to rest as dark approached.

"I am thirsty," Tuta complained, looking down on the black ribbon of water at the bottom of the valley. Mato gave her young some of the stale, warm water that she had carried since morning.

Shutok and Yaiya refused the waterskin when Ala held it out to them. "You should drink," she told her sons. "And you should stop this foolishness before someone is hurt. You are not hunters yet, and this is a dangerous game you are playing."

"I am not thirsty."

Ala shook her head disapprovingly at Yaiya and offered the skin once more to Shutok.

"Nor am I."

Ala tied the neck of the skin shut and Shutok looked away. The horizon was low and flat, with no landmarks. The sky was black and the earth was blacker, that was all, and Shutok had no way of telling how far he had run today. The river was still a long way off, but he could see it, and when the wind was right he thought he could hear fresh water and smell it. Neither he nor Yaiya would drink until the hunters did.

"We will go on then," Aar said. He spoke scornfully, impatient with the delay.

Yaiya jumped to his feet with a display of energy and Shutok hoped his brother would not notice the difficulty he had standing. The boys shouldered their burdens and set off downhill together.

In front of them the hunters bounded down the slope like antelope, weightless and free, but descending was an ordeal for Shutok, worse than running on the open prairie. Pain shot through his left leg with each jolting step. It was as if he had walked on a cactus thorn, except the thorn went deep behind his knee and up past his hip to a burning spot low in the center of his back.

"You are tired." Shutok was surprised to hear his mother's voice so close behind him and he turned to look at her. In the darkness she was vague, part of the night, and he was uncomfortable.

"No," he said, and kept walking. Ahead of him Yaiya had slowed down to listen.

"It is not like Aar to decide that we must be at the river tonight," she said. "Why must we travel on so black a night? And who knows what lies waiting there or there? The killer of men, perhaps?"

"And you are not feeling well," Yaiya observed.

"I feel all right," Shutok insisted. "What makes you think there is anything wrong? I have kept up with you all day, so what could be wrong?"

"Maybe that's why Aar decided to run to the river," he suggested. "To find out."

Shutok pitched on more recklessly after that, but he arrived at the river behind everyone else. He found them sitting next to the water with their burdens unopened beside them. The water was good and he told himself that he was glad he had waited to drink. The only thing bad about this place was the mosquitoes. They swarmed around him and flew into his mouth and nose as he breathed. A smoky fire would keep them away, he thought, and they could cover themselves with skins for shelter. But the others had not begun to make a camp.

Aar and the other two hunters straightened and Shutok understood that they were going on. They had been waiting for him. He was not given time to rest — the mosquitoes made them all eager to go. Quietly the boy asked his mother how much farther.

"Didn't you see the village just there?" she said, pointing upriver. His eyes had been on his feet, searching the dark hillside for the easiest way down. "These people are friendly, although they are not of the way. They do not hunt as we do. Instead they fish," she said disgustedly, "and kill the bison from boats as they swim across the river. We do not respect them, but they are friendly. We will stay in their camp tonight. It is not far."

They walked as one group, the women and children staying close to the hunters so that the river people would see that they were not interested in fighting. Pathways cut by the wind led them between clumps of dense brush. They smelled smoke, and they heard dogs. Then, round-ing a corner in the maze of brush, they saw the village. In the dark, the brush houses of the river people looked like the rest of the riverbank, and Aar seemed worried that they had come so close. Except for the barking of the dogs and the cries of an infant, there was an alarming silence from the village.

"Stop," he said. "We will wait here." Words were for women and children; hunters spoke among themselves in a language of their own, a language of the eyes and of action, and with barely a perceptible gesture Aar instructed the other hunters, Gan and Hnit, to watch their flanks. The river people stood apart, absorbed by the night. More of them might be moving just out of sight to surround the little band.

Finally, as if after waiting for just that, one of the villagers stepped forward to parley.

"Look," Ala whispered. Even in the dark it was obvious that something was wrong with the stocky man who had indicated he wanted to talk. His skin was scaly and discolored. "See what evil befalls those who are not of our way!" she said.

The man did not come any closer than he had to in order to be seen. "Who are you and what do you want?" he asked, using the sign language of the prairies.

"We are the wolf people," Aar answered, like the man using his hands instead of his voice. "We have come into your village before as friends. Do you not remember?"

"What do you want here?"

"We have come to pick up the shiny black rocks, and tonight we would like to share your fires."

When Aar signed that they would like to come into the village, the men standing in the dark spoke among themselves in their own language. Shutok could feel their attitude grow more threatening.

"Do you have something to trade for the rocks and for the fire?" the man signed. "Others have come saying the same thing, only to steal from us like coyotes."

Aar drew himself up at this insult, and behind him Ala bristled, speaking loudly to Mato. "Now what would we have with us to trade?" she spat. "What have you carried all day to trade with these fish eaters, Mato? We are hunters, not fishermen. To hunt, the wolf carries nothing."

"And to share a fire, or pick up stones from the earth, we are called coyotes!" Mato replied. "Who would expect such a thing? But our hunters will not lose face like this." She pulled Tuta close to her and kept a hand on him. The council was over, the women clearly having had their say, and now all of them waited for Aar's decision.

He signaled for Ala, Mato, and Tuta to withdraw.

"Now I will show the hunters that I am no boy," Yaiya said to his younger brother. Shutok felt unsteady on his feet. By matching each man with one of his fingers he discovered that there were more of the enemy than anyone could count.

"You and I have no weapons," he reminded Yaiya. "We must not fight with them." Yaiya snorted in a way that was meant to be scornful of his brother's caution. Shutok thought he sounded scared.

When enough time had passed for Ala, Mato, and Tuta

to get to the shelter of the brush, the hunters tried to back away with dignity, shouting insults at the river people.

"Fish eaters!" Shutok joined in, knowing that the villagers would only understand how he said it, not what he said. "You even look and smell like fish." He backed away, holding himself erect, but with a filthy expression on his face, as if the enemy were not dangerous, but disgusting. The river men did not come after them, but they jeered back from all sides.

Then Shutok tripped. The fall was startling and the boy cried out in fear and pain. Though knowing better, he felt as if he had been hit with a spear. He got to his feet and ran after the hunters, his left leg withering under him every time he put his weight on it. Ahead of him the three men and Yaiya faded away into the night like bright stones dropped into black water.

"Where is Shutok?" he heard Yaiya say. Then they were gone, and the boy thought he would be captured. He crawled into the brush and waited. Men were shouting, dogs barking. A voice near him said something in a language that was frightful gibberish and a dark shape bent to retrieve a spear from the sand. Even after the voices went back into the village, Shutok dared not move, even to drive away the mosquitoes that tormented him. Only when there were no sounds from the village did he leave his hiding place to sneak downstream.

Thorny hillocks surrounded him. Shutok walked between them, hearing the river to his right, but he was confused by blind meanderings and dead ends. When he tried heading straight for the sound of water the brush cut him and he gave it up. Testing the uneven, black ground with his right foot, then dragging his left up behind it, painfully, slowly, he kept on until he thought he would have to stop walking and crawl. After what seemed like the entire night he found the spot by the river where the others had waited for him earlier, and he realized with a shock that they were not there now.

"Ala?" he said, hardly louder than a whisper. "Yaiya?" He crawled along the river for a short distance, then came back. They were nowhere near.

"They left me!" he said to himself in disbelief. Perhaps they blamed him for the disgrace of running from an enemy. They ran only after he cried out, and Ala had warned him that they would blame him for anything that went wrong. Or maybe they thought he had been killed or captured.

He tried to decide what to do. He had never spent a night alone. He was too young for that. Even when he was older, and was sent onto the prairie alone to find his power, he would be allowed to make a fire to protect himself from the ones who hunted at night. And he had dropped his burden, so he did not have his robe — not that it was cold. Mosquitoes! They coated him like feathers, clinging to him even if he waved his arms about madly. He wanted to run from them, but he couldn't. He decided to stay put.

Shutok threw a layer of sand over his body to keep off the mosquitoes. There were stars to see by but no moon.

He listened fearfully, hearing nothing but the river and the wretched buzz of mosquitoes.

The sounds that woke him were comforting until he opened his eyes and remembered where he was. They were human sounds. Someone was singing nearby, as if to himself, for the song broke off, then started again, stopped. The song and the language were not his people's. This was an enemy.

He lay perfectly still, only his head showing above the blanket of sand. The evil was there next to his spine like a stone. Just his eyes moved as he searched for the singer, although in his mind and heart he ran.

When he first saw her she was walking bent over his tracks like the foolish hunter in one of Aar's stories who stalked the bear's pawprints as if they were the bear. The girl had the same disease Ala had noticed the night before. Her skin, even her face, looked like dried mud, and it was only after she was almost upon him that he realized it was mud, to keep the mosquitoes from biting.

She was not armed, close to Shutok's size. Perhaps bigger, he thought, looking up at her. She might easily have walked on him. At the very last step she looked up, saw his head lying detached in the sand, and stopped. With fear and surprise and curiosity in her wide eyes all at the same time she looked like a doe about to spring away.

Because he remembered Aar's story about the hunter who became a meal for the bear, Shutok bared his teeth at the girl and growled his fiercest. She jumped so high that she came down off balance and fell in a heap on the ground.

As she struggled to her feet Shutok's fear left him. He laughed at her, causing the sand to slide off his body. The girl did not stop running until she was out of reach of a spear thrown from the strongest arm. Shutok could see her dark head as she peered at him from behind a ridge of brush and sand, so he growled again and then laughed even harder.

"Dirty face!" he teased.

Shutok stood and brushed the sand off himself. Standing was awkward and painful, although not as bad as the night before. There was a faint line of footprints in the sand. He began following it downriver, thinking of the distance that even now might be widening between him and his people. If they had crossed the river this morning he might never catch them.

His one hope was that a kill would be made. The band sometimes stayed three or four days at a kill, until the meat began to spoil or until predators or scavengers made lingering either dangerous or disagreeable. Then they would wrap what was needed for survival in their burden bundles and set off in pursuit of the herds again. In the north, many walks from this river, there was another land where they dared not travel. They would stay all summer in a cave at the edge of a huge marsh and wait for the bison to return in the fall. It was a good place to stay, and when he got there he would drive this evil from him once and for all.

Shutok lengthened his stride and fell down with a whimper. He had gotten carried away, he thought, so he decided to rest. Looking back to see how far he had come, he saw a dark head disappear behind a clump of brush.

"What are you following me for?" he yelled back to her. "Stupid girl! Go home!"

The boy started walking with cautious determination, but at a bend in the river where the bank was cut away the ground was too rough and rocky. Afraid he might fall, he decided to crawl until he came to easier ground.

The girl came closer. He growled again. It no longer worked.

Shutok came to smoother ground and he walked. Looking over his shoulder he saw the girl pick up a stick of driftwood. She was getting too close so he tried to walk faster.

It was no surprise when the blow came, knocking him to the ground, flat, and taking his breath away. He lay gulping for air. She had hit him from behind and then run.

"Coward!" he yelled when he got his breath back. "Stay away from me." He got to his hands and knees and crawled on.

The second time he heard her steps coming toward him, he turned to face her. Shutok growled again and raised an arm to fend off the attack. She hit him squarely on the shoulder. Shutok squealed in outrage and fear, afraid she was going to beat him to death.

"Grrr!" She stood before him bravely now, growling as he had done. She raised the stick as if to hit him, but laughed instead. Shutok put on a face of stone. It was the way. A hunter faced a humiliating death without wincing.

But instead of killing him the girl pointed upriver. To make sure he understood she hit him again. Shutok began crawling in his own tracks back toward the village.

His hands and knees were sore and he was not moving fast. The girl seemed patient, stooping now and then to pick up sticks of firewood, so he crawled even slower. Although he felt in his heart that it was useless, he stalled. He stopped to rest.

The girl growled at him and then gave him a solid whack across the small of his back. The pain made him catch his breath, but he felt such rage when she laughed at him that he made a desperate grab for her ankles. She was too quick for him.

"Go ahead," he said. "Hit me again if you want. I won't go any farther."

She looked at him quizzically, her head tilted slightly like a sassy bird's. The girl said something that he could not understand, but at least she was not hitting him.

"Why don't you let me go? I am no good to anyone as a slave. Look at me. I can't even walk. Your people will kill me rather than feed me."

Then she hit him.

"Beat me to death here and now! I am not afraid, and I won't let you disgrace me any more. I won't crawl to a sure death."

He sat there and she hit him again. The girl said something that sounded like an order and Shutok knew what she meant. She raised the stick a third time before Shutok changed his mind and started to crawl. She laughed, but not with any humor in her voice. The joke was getting old.

"Ugly!" he shouted.

Then someone else laughed and it was a man's voice. Shutok collapsed.

So it was over, he thought. They could not be very near to the village yet, but someone must have come looking for her. Now he was a captive and the girl's cruelty had only been the beginning. He felt tears forming and he fought them unsuccessfully. The shame of crying before an enemy was going to be part of his disgrace.

When he heard a second laugh, Shutok was not much relieved to recognize it as Yaiya's.

The girl did not seem to know what to do until she saw the three men and Yaiya step out into the open. They were good hunters and they had surrounded her without her knowing it.

It was hopeless, but the girl ran. She struggled in Aar's arms when he brought her back to where Shutok lay exhausted in the sand.

"Look," Yaiya said. "There is no wound. What have we come back for? Shutok has grown two more legs, and from now on we will hear him howling at the moon like a coyote and sneaking around our camp for scraps."

"Shut up!" The stick was beside him, and Shutok picked it up. Yaiya stepped back with a laugh.

"Hold her," Shutok said. He wanted to beat the girl but the evil in his back had grown so powerful that he was able to hit her just once in the shins.

"So THERE YOU ARE. Ala sent me to look for you."

"How much farther?" For days and days Shutok had asked himself that question with each paralyzing twinge. Any slight turning or bending could set off the spasms in his back and leg. It felt like hitting his elbow, that same sickening tingle and the same helplessness to make it stop, except this pain was larger and closer to the edge of the unendurable.

"Can you see just over there?"

"No." Shutok was on his hands and knees again. He could not see over the grasses.

"Not far. Let me help you up," Yaiya said. Then in another voice he added, "Look at that!" He meant Shutok's palms and kneecaps. They were open, dirty sores. "Can't you walk at all?"

"Yes, I can walk, but only for a short way. Then I stumble, or turn to look at something. Anything I do makes the evil in my back angry. When I crawl it is not so bad. Easy!"

Yaiya supported his brother from the left side and made an apologetic face as they tried to walk together.

"Slower, slower!" Shutok said urgently. It went better after Yaiya understood his brother's halting, foot-dragging step and let Shutok lead.

"How long have you been looking for me?"

"All afternoon. We stopped just after the sun was highest in the sky. We waited a long time and then Aar told us to make camp. He was angry again. We have come so short a distance today that we can see the buzzards over the last kill."

Once more Shutok promised, "It will be better tomorrow." He had been promising as much since the river, but because of the girl the hunters would not stop to rest. They were still worried about the villagers, who might come after her.

"Will you . . . ?" But then Shutok thought better of the question. How could he ask Yaiya to stay behind with him the next day, to help, when he knew how important it was to his brother to show the hunters that he was strong enough to run with them?

"What?"

"Nothing. It was nothing. I will feel better tomorrow."

"They did not hunt today. It is too soon after the last kill. You know we will not rest tomorrow, and Aar says we must move quickly or we will be left here with nothing to hunt when the bison are gone."

"Yes, I know. But I can keep up somehow." They were getting close to camp and Yaiya hurried him too much. A cry escaped Shutok's throat and then he said, "I can walk from here."

"No. I am sorry if I hurt you. We can go slower."

"How many walks to the marsh, do you know?"

"No. Many, many walks, and long ones too. Aar told us today that you will not make it. He said that we must go on without you."

"I will make it."

The three hunters talked among themselves when Yaiya and Shutok walked into camp. Shutok knew what they were saying. Nothing good about him, that was certain. He had caused them to lose face at the river — they ran after he fell because they thought the villagers were attacking. Capturing the girl had helped them to regain some of their self-respect. Nevertheless, Aar spoke slightingly of the girl, saying, "A dog would be more useful than another mouth to feed when the hungry time comes again."

Yaiya helped Shutok as far as their mother. Ala's eyes took everything in with such a sadness that Shutok felt sorry for her. She was sitting with the slave girl, who watched Shutok carefully. A leather strap was tied around her neck but she was not staked down. Only five short walks from the river, the boy noted sullenly, and already they trusted her to walk around in camp.

"It is bad," Ala stated without moving. "Yaiya, bring the waterskin and food."

"Sh . . . Shutok!" The boy turned his head. It was the slave girl who had spoken his name. He raised his hand to slap her, but Ala stopped him.

"That's right, that's right," Ala told the girl, patting her hand and smiling. "If she is to be a good slave she must learn the right way to talk and forget that terrible noise her people make. She knows everyone's name now," and to prove it Ala had the girl recite them.

"Who is the other woman?" Ala asked, pointing, and the girl answered, "Mato."

"Who is Mato's little boy?"

"Tuta."

"And the hunter who is Mato's man, our leader?" Ala pointed again.

"Aar."

"My man is named . . ."

"Gan."

The girl had trouble remembering Hnit, the third hunter, but she smiled broadly when it was her turn to recite the names of Yaiya, Ala, and Shutok. "See what a fast learner she is?" Ala boasted.

"But it is her fault that I cannot walk," Shutok said bitterly. "If she had not beaten me nearly to death I wouldn't be like this."

"Perhaps. But I think it was bad before. Is there no way you can move faster? The hunters . . ."

"Yaiya told me."

"I cannot send him back to get you tomorrow. You will have to move faster and keep up on your own. You know it is the way. Can you remember when we had to leave old Minot?" Ala paused as if to give him time to remember, but Shutok had not forgotten. They had abandoned Minot two seasons ago when the ancient woman could no longer walk.

"It is the same now. The hunters have been patient

because there are so few of us. We need young to become hunters. But if we wait here too long we will starve later on when the herds go into the lands of our enemies."

"I understand," Shutok said evenly, then in a defiant voice he added, "I will make it. Wait and see!"

But Shutok's determination only brought tears to his mother's eyes.

In the morning Mato did not sing to Tuta as they picked up after each other. She was solemn and she shushed the boy whenever he started to talk. Ala was distracted with the girl. She had told Shutok what the girl's name was, but it was not anything that he could remember. Yaiya was off by himself. Only the hunters were no different than they always were. They sat on their heels silently and apart from the others, eager to start. Everyone knew what was happening, and in their manner they showed their sadness, so there was no need to say anything. Shutok remembered leaving Minot, and this was the way they had said good-bye to her.

Shutok found Yaiya. He watched with curiosity as his brother cut up his robe. It was the skin he wrapped up to make his burden bundle. He was secretive, and Shutok left without saying anything to him.

They all started together but Shutok was slower and they soon left him behind. Yaiya stayed with him just a little longer than the others. He handed Shutok the scraps of hide that he had cut from his robe.

"Your hands and knees," he said, and Shutok understood. "I heard the hunters talking. Aar said that we will stay in a high place and keep the fire bright." Then Yaiya took off to catch the others.

Shutok wanted to shout something cheerful after his brother, but he stopped himself with his hand up in the air. It seemed out of place, so he focused his attention on the ground beneath his feet.

The grasses came up to the boy's waist, hiding his footing. The prairie, which seemed so flat to the eye, was like a shallow lake covering a rugged bottom. Bunch grass roots raised the ground in clumps. Shutok felt his way between them with his right foot, sometimes placing it several times before bringing his left up to a level resting place. It was like walking in the dark, except that as long as he was standing he could see over the grass. As long as he could look up and see his family he was not alone and he was not lost.

Shutok came upon a prairie dog colony and saw footprints where those ahead of him had stepped through the animal's shallow tunnels. He would need to crawl to avoid falling.

At least here the prairie dogs ate the grass down short, and there was open dirt in places, especially around their mounded burrows. But it was impossible to tell how far he would have to crawl before he could safely walk again. Some prairie dog colonies were bigger than people could walk across in one day.

The boy had no solitude here. Sharp warning calls shot out from disturbed prairie dogs half in and half out of their burrows, while others that he passed barked out an "all clear" while standing on their hind legs.

There were prairie dogs as far as Shutok could see in every direction, but other animals were in the colony as well. He saw a hawk gliding over the ground like a flat rock skipped across a smooth pond, and once a coyote looked him over with suspicion. The antelope and the bison liked it here, for it was a place to roll and kick in bare, dry dirt. The boy knew there could be others. Wolves and rattlesnakes hunted prairie dogs and used abandoned burrows for dens. This would be a terrifying place to cross at night, he thought.

Yaiya's scraps of hide worked well for Shutok, although they would not stay in place on his knees unless he tied them so tightly around his legs that his feet tingled. Still, kneecaps and hands were not for walking on; the aches in his shoulders and legs, when he spotted the camp and straightened himself up to walk the final distance, seemed worse than the ache in his back.

Surprise was obvious even on the faces of the hunters, but the slave girl was the only one who expressed it. "Shutok?" she said, "Shutok?" She made it sound as if she had been expecting someone else.

But of course, they were surprised only because they were not expecting anyone. They did not congratulate him or encourage him. Their awkwardness hurt Shutok more than anything. "They still don't think I can do it," he muttered to himself. "And it isn't even dark yet. I made good today."

But there was no prairie dog colony to make Shutok's traveling easier the next day. Night caught him far from camp. He was guided by the flicker of the fire, in a high place and burning brightly, just as Aar had said it would be, but always seeming closer than it was.

The grass at night was full of movement, and Shutok's every sense kept asking, "What was that?" until his neck muscles stiffened into a headache. He had to fight the voice in him that told him to hide there, rest, and go the remainder of the way in the morning.

"I've got to go on," he told that voice, "or I will just be that much farther behind tomorrow."

Not even the girl remarked on his entrance into camp that night. She was snuggled next to Ala, the strap gone from around her neck. Shutok crawled close to his brother and slept without eating or drinking.

Then, like the flushing of a bird from a bush, another night was gone. Shutok knew that it was morning already, and that the others were leaving, but he felt so secure here and sleep was so welcoming that he drifted off again.

He woke with a start, thinking to himself that this would be how it happened. He would lose his determination and be left behind. But beside him, where he was sure to notice them, Yaiya had left Shutok some food and new kneepads.

"Another dare, is it? Well, I can keep up with you." He ate quickly and set off.

Shutok stopped thinking about anything but moving as fast as possible, bent on getting to camp before dark. How many more walks would there be before they came to the marsh? The prairie seemed endless, but then he would remember the food and the kneepads that Yaiya had left for him, and Shutok drove himself on.

The sun was already low in the sky when he realized that he had lost all traces of his family. Where had he last seen them? He thought it must have been at the bottom of the low, rolling hill off to his right, but he was not sure now. There were other swells and dips in the landscape and they all looked very much alike. Scanning the horizon in every direction for movement, he saw only grass, darkened in huge patches here and there by the shadows of clouds.

"Nothing to worry about," he comforted himself. He would be able to see their fire. Shutok set off toward the hillside where he thought he had last seen them.

It was dusk by the time he was able to see around the rise. Nothing — just prairie and more prairie — but Shutok still did not think that he was lost. It was too early yet for a fire to show up brightly.

"They must have come through here somewhere," he mused. He decided that he would continue as long as he had light. It would put him that much closer to camp when he finally was able to see the fire.

Shutok had taken only a few steps when a prairie hen flew from her nest, right beneath his feet, setting the boy's senses into a frenzy of alarm. He tried to laugh it off, but it was growing dark and his panic was difficult to control. Night was the time when man-killers hunted.

Where was the fire?

Wondering what else he could do, he sat down on the spot. The nest had eggs in it, but the boy was too discouraged to think of eating them.

In the morning the buzzards and the smoke were unmistakable, but that hardly mattered to Shutok. He could see that they must be camped near a kill, just out of sight around another hillside. He had given up too soon, that was all, but he felt that he was going to have to give up once and for all. He had been stubborn, but this was as good a place as any to wait for the inevitable.

His stomach groaned when he looked at the prairie hen's eggs. Three of them were good, but after eating them he felt hungrier. Every part of his body, inside and out, hurt. He lay on his back, his raw knees pulled up so that his back was not so painful, but lying like that only made his stomach complain more. Shutok started to crawl, almost angry with himself for being so foolish.

Again and again he stopped. Even after he could see them he wondered if he was going to make it and why he should try. Shutok promised himself that this would be his last camp. When they left him this time, he would stay.

Suddenly he heard something prowling through the grass just to his left. As weak as he was, his fear of death was still strong and he flattened himself against the ground.

"Shutok?" It was the girl. The boy's fear was still with him, for she had seen him and she was walking toward him with a stick in her hands.

"Shutok?" She was calling him so that she could beat him out of sight of the others, he thought.

Standing over him she seemed to know what he was thinking. "No, Shutok," she said. With the stick under her arm she did some sort of dance, walking with three legs instead of two.

"Leave me alone," he pleaded. "Can't I die without your craziness?"

"No, Shutok," and she danced some more. Then she seemed to understand that he did not know what she was doing, and did not care. She said something quietly in her own language.

"Go away. Haven't you done enough to me?"

She helped him to his feet, more gently than Yaiya had done. After she walked him into camp, the girl went back for the stick she had left behind.

"SHUTOK. SHUTOK. SHUTOK." Like a bird singing its song identically again and again the girl stood over him repeating his name. Shutok opened his eyes and looked up at her with a sour expression on his face.

"What do you want now, Uita?" He had heard Ala call her that this morning, and he saw that he had remembered her name correctly. Even when her eyes smiled like this, though, there was something about them that made Shutok distrust her. He was too tired to care what it was.

"Stick," she announced, holding it out to him.

"Yes, that's right," he said, as if speaking to a baby. He remembered Tuta at a stage like this. "Rock," he would say, going around to everyone and showing it. "Mato," pointing to her. "Mato rock." But he had stopped talking like that a long time ago. This girl was as old as Shutok, making the boy wonder if all the river people were this stupid.

"You are learning," he said. "But I am not your teacher. Ala is over there. Go away and leave me alone."

"Shutok stick."

"Thank you. Now go away." But she did not go away.

When he opened his eyes again she was still there. He watched her put the forked end of the stick under her arm and dance with it. Then she wanted him to try, holding it out to him. It was silly. Did she want to play?

Shutok knew the others were watching, although when he looked at them they turned their eyes aside as if in embarrassment. The day before they had given him up for dead, and Uita seemed to be the only one not to understand that it was best not to offer any false encouragement. She was troubling them, too, by pestering him, but they did nothing to stop her. Uita put her hand under his arm to help him stand.

"Oh, all right then," he submitted. He wanted a drink anyway. The stiffness in his joints made him lean heavily on her and he was frightened. Uita balanced him and put the stick under his left arm.

"Wait!" he protested when she let go of him. She held her arms out, ready to catch him if he toppled, but he did not fall.

Instead, it seemed to lift him. Standing straight, with the brittle stoop forced out of his back by the unbending crutch, Shutok was taller than he had believed himself to be. Like a spear-thrower, which in a hunter's hand became an extension of his arm and muscle, this stick was at once part of Shutok and yet so strangely powerful that the boy was awed by it. It was as if he could suddenly hold fire or light in the palm of his hand.

He looked from the girl to the others, but he could not interpret the look on their faces. Their eyes were on

34

the crutch, watching it as if anything might happen.

Shutok timidly placed his right foot forward. He moved the crutch next, then his left foot. It was almost painless, so he repeated the sequence. The third time he tried it his left foot barely touched the ground, and the magic of the stick was his. The others watched him walk to the water-hole and back, and when they left the kill two days later, Shutok went after them.

One day many walks later Yaiya told him, "The hunters say they have never seen such a thing before. This stick is something magic, to cure you like this."

"The evil is still there," Shutok told him. But he did not deny that the stick was magic. A walking stick was a common thing, but this stick fit under his arm and took the place of the leg that would not hold his weight. Whether good or bad, he thought, surely to know of such a thing the girl must have spirit-medicine.

But even with the help of the stick, Shutok's plodding between camps was seldom finished before dark. By wrapping hide around the fork that went beneath his arm he made the stick more comfortable, but walking was hard and slow and lonely.

Yaiya went with the hunters, although he could not hunt. He had not been sent after power, but there was no question that he had been accepted as one of their group. And Ala had adopted Uita. They walked together, Ala teaching her the words for things by pointing and having the girl repeat what she said. Even Mato, pregnant and with Tuta in tow, outwalked Shutok. At the end of each day he hoped that the next walk would bring them to the marsh, where he could stop.

Then one morning the girl was singing the song he remembered from the river. Ala asked Mato, "And did you sleep well last night?"

"No," Mato replied with a smile. "The mosquitoes kept me awake."

"Perhaps no one will sleep tonight," Ala said, and they both laughed. Shutok looked at the girl. She was throwing dirt all over herself as she sang. Mosquitoes meant water, and Shutok shared their excitement, but for someone to say that today they would see the marsh would only disappoint them if they were mistaken.

The boy walked that day with his eyes focused on the ground, not wanting to look up only to see more prairie. There was nothing he could do to make the distance go by faster. It seemed the longest walk yet, but that afternoon he stood alone on the rimrock overlooking the marsh. On the far side of it was the cave. In just a day or two he could stop.

"Yo-ho-ho-o," he let loose, but the victory cry sounded empty and false because no one was close enough to share it with him.

The rimrock faced south and it collected the sun's heat. The morning of his first day of rest Shutok let the heat soak into his back, but in the afternoon when it became too hot he moved inside the cave where it was cooler. He lay down again just inside the shadow of the roof, beneath the lowest corner of the entrance.

"I do not like this," Ala was saying. The two women and Uita were working to clean up the mess they had found the day before, but the signs were still plain enough for anyone to see, even after they had walked over most of the tracks and had cleared away the bones that had littered the floor of the cave.

"At least it looks as if it has gone away," Mato commented. "It only stayed here during the winter."

"But it was never here before. I don't like it. Never has there been anything here but us."

"There was the builder of the nest," Shutok said, but they ignored him. No one liked to talk about the nest because no one knew what had made it. Aar told them never to move any part of the great pile of sticks because the spirit of the animal that made it might be insulted and return. It must have been a beast larger than a bison, for the wood choked the back of the cave to the height of a man.

But Ala and Mato were concerned about this new cave-dweller, not the ancient one.

"This cave would be a good place to stay the winter," Mato continued. "I am surprised that such a one does not live here every winter. But it has moved out in time for us."

"There is too much smoke in here for most animals to like it. Look, it is baked into the walls and ceiling. It always smells of smoke. No, only the killer of men is so daring. And this one is big, bigger maybe than anyone has ever seen before. Look at the size of those pawprints."

"But they are old ones. The bones it left were nearly

dry. It has been gone for a long time and it will probably not return until it snows."

"Let us hope not," Ala answered her. "With Yaiya soon to go after power, I do not like the thought of a sharp-toothed one in the marsh."

The cat's tracks made Shutok nervous for Yaiya, too. From his corner in the mouth of the cave he could see down into part of the marsh, an eerie place even without the menace of a man-hunter — this cat that they talked about only in a roundabout way. Its name was a forbidden word, and the boy did not say it even in his thoughts for fear that the cougar — if that was what had left such huge pawprints — might hear it and come.

"But we are not people of the marsh. Won't Aar send Yaiya out onto the prairie?" Shutok asked. It was hard to see the women in the gloomy cave after looking out into the bright sunlight and he closed his eyes for a moment.

"It is too far," Ala answered. "We made three walks to get here around the edge of the marsh, and on the other side of us, to the north, is the land of our enemies. Aar will send him into the marsh."

"Are the people who live in the marsh friendly?"

"They are a cowardly people. They have boats made of reeds and they disappear into the marsh if we come too close. If they see Yaiya they will stay away from him."

The women talked some more, but Shutok kept his eyes closed and let their voices lull him into sleep. He had nothing to do now that they were here, and for days and days he rested, hoping that he would build up the strength he needed to resist the evil in his back. It stopped hurting when he was idle, and he thought that he was healing fast enough, until one day he happened to overhear Mato and Tuta talking about him.

"Why won't Shutok help us any more?" the boy asked his mother. It was during the hottest time of the day and they were walking up the path from the creek with full waterskins. The slope between the cave and the creek was open to the sun, but cottonwoods and several large boulders provided shade beside the water and Shutok liked to lie there. The breeze that followed the creek down its little valley was cool even on the warmest days, although the mosquitoes were as bad there as anywhere else.

"It is sad to watch, but Shutok is doomed," she answered.

"What does that mean?"

"It means that he should have died on the prairie, for he will die sooner or later. As long as he hangs on like this it only makes it harder on everyone else. He has an evil spirit in him that could bring us all bad luck."

"Then why did Uita give him that stick?"

"Because she does not know our way. Maybe among her people the sick ones and the old people are allowed to live. We cannot stay in the same place all the time, so when the sick and the old can no longer walk with us we have to leave them."

"But we will stay here, so it is all right that he stays here with us, isn't it?"

"Yes, it is all right as long as there is enough food for everyone. But he is not getting better. He does not do his share of the work now. What will happen when the bison return and we have to leave again?"

"We will leave him here?"

"Yes, we will leave him here."

"And he will die?"

"Yes. That is the way."

In the days that followed, Shutok went for water and he gathered firewood. He felt like an outcast after hearing what Mato had said about him. The women did not use much fuel in the warm weather, so after a day or two the wood he brought went into a pile outside the cave. He made trip after trip down the hill and along the creek even after it was obvious that there was enough wood to last for more days than anyone could count. His woodpile began to look like the nest-builder's pile in the back of the cave. But if his work made any difference in the attitudes of the others, they did not show it.

Shutok concentrated hard on bending and lifting carefully so he would not arouse the evil. He used his left hand on his crutch and dragged the wood back to camp. It was easier than trying to carry an awkward load with one hand.

As careful as he was, however, the evil was there like an enemy. Shutok spoke soothingly to it as if it were someone he could reason with. Whenever he made a false move the grinding and pinching in his back and leg made him clench his teeth. Then he apologized to it, trying anything to make it stop hurting.

One day he dropped the branch he was dragging. "All right," he said, speaking to the twinges in his back. "All right, I will look for a smaller one."

"Uita will help Shutok," he heard. He turned in time

to see her step nimbly from stone to stone across the creek. She bent to pick up the end of the branch.

"No," he said. "Leave it there."

She straightened up and Shutok saw that one of her eyes pointed off to the side, like a bird's. It was slight but noticeable, and he wondered why he had never seen it before. He could not tell which eye was looking at him so he looked at her mouth.

"Shutok does not want it?" she asked. Ala had taught her many words in a short time, but the way she said them always sounded odd.

"Yes," he said irritably. "I want it, but I don't need any help from you, or anybody else, either. I can do my share." He could see by the puzzled look on her face that he had spoken too fast. He bent to get the branch and woke the evil. The pain made him furious with Uita.

"Go away!" he yelled at her. "I hate you, you cross-eyed..." He broke off because he could not think of anything bad enough to call her, but the girl understood the tone of his voice and left him alone. He had hurt her feelings and he was glad of it. That afternoon when he dropped the big branch beside his woodpile, Shutok felt that he had won an important victory over Uita. And Mato, too, he thought, looking at the size of the pile.

He looked for big pieces after that, going farther and farther downstream to find them. It was slower, harder work, but until the evenings became cooler he was able to keep his woodpile growing.

Then one day he found something that took some of his time away from wood gathering. He was pulling another large branch across the creek when he stumbled and fell into the shallow water. It hurt until he got to the bank where he sat resting, tossing pebbles into the stream. A stone shining on the bottom of the creek caught his eye and he picked it up.

It was a flake of obsidian bigger than his hand. The glassy black stone had to have been carried there by someone and dropped, for this type of rock was not to be found near the marsh. The only place Shutok had seen obsidian was along the river where they had fought with Uita's people.

When he held it up to the sun, the light shone dully through the stone where it was thin around the edges, and he rotated it slowly to see the lines, gray and black, that gave this piece its character. He thought it was the most beautiful stone he had ever seen. Aar, whose points were delicate and so finely shaped that even the broken ones that littered their camps were things to be picked up and studied, would appreciate it when Shutok gave it to him.

"Are you hurt?" Shutok was shocked by the voice and his first impulse was to hide the stone, but then he saw that it was his brother.

"Come see what I found here in the water," Shutok called to him. He and Yaiya had not been close this summer. Yaiya spent most of his time with the hunters, but even when he was in camp, Shutok had the idea that his brother avoided him. Yaiya, of course, wanted to seem grown up, and it was not fitting for him to be seen with Shutok.

"I was following a grouse when I saw you fall," he said. "And then when I came back and saw that you were still here I thought I had better see if you were hurt. What have you got there, obsidian?" He sat down next to Shutok and held the stone up to the light when it was handed to him.

"Did you get the grouse?"

"With a pointed stick?" Yaiya said disgustedly. "I needed a spear-thrower. Why won't they send me on my power journey? I am tired of play-hunting like a boy."

"They will send you soon. I am sure of it," Shutok said cheerfully. He did not like to see this scowl on his brother's face. It usually meant that Yaiya was trying to think of something to do. Whatever he came up with was bound to land them both in trouble.

"But we have been here how long now? I have watched the moon and it will be full again in just a few more nights. Two moons and they have not sent me!"

"There is time yet. The bison will not come back until it gets cold. The leaves will fall from the trees first and then we will go."

Handing the stone back to his brother, Yaiya asked, "What will you do with this?"

"Give it to the hunters, what else?"

Yaiya looked at him slyly before he made his suggestion. "You could give it to me," he said.

Shutok was a little too long in responding and the scowl returned to Yaiya's face. "What will you do with it?"

He should not have asked. Yaiya hotly refused it when he tried to give it to him now. "Here," Shutok insisted.

"I am sure that you will not break the way. It would bring bad luck to you when you go to find power."

"And what if I did break the way? Who would have to know? Certainly you are not going to tell the hunters if I make a point out of the stone. They are about to drive you off like an outcast anyway, and telling them will only make them do it sooner." Yaiya, when he was arguing with Shutok about something he wanted, could hurt his brother's feelings seemingly without a second thought.

"Of course I wouldn't say anything. But you know what they would think if they did happen to find out about it. They would think that you are a coward. I know that you are not afraid to go without a weapon."

"And what would they think if I returned wearing the pelt of the killer of men?" So that was it. Yaiya wanted to hunt the animal that had been living in the cave. "I cannot kill it with a pointed stick. And you should be thinking about what is going to happen to you. You know that you cannot go with us when we leave here. You have to plan for that. Don't you think that you will need a weapon of your own? Split the stone with me. We will both make spear points out of it."

Shutok knew that Yaiya was not thinking of him at all, but somehow that did not matter. This was how it had always been between them — Yaiya scheming and Shutok following — and Shutok realized almost with tears that this might be the last time. Yaiya would soon be a hunter.

He gave in, and they split the stone by striking it sharply with another rock.

THE BOYS NEEDED A private place where they could shape
their pieces of obsidian into points without fear of being
caught, and Shutok knew just the right spot. It was on
the far side of the creek in a small sandy clearing low on
the hillside facing the cave. There were two big boulders
in the clearing and trees around it for shade. They could
watch the path between the waterhole and the cave from
there while staying out of sight themselves.

After working two afternoons on their obsidian they
were both disappointed that it was not as easy as the
hunters made it look.

"This isn't turning out right at all," Yaiya said in exas-
peration. "I can see the shape clearly in my mind but I
can't get it to come out." He was out of sorts again today.
The moon had been full the night before, and Yaiya was
so eager to be a hunter that he could hardly sit still long
enough to get a single chip to flake away from his stone
before he stood up to pace around the clearing.

"I know what you mean," Shutok agreed. "It is like it
is there, waiting in the rock. But the important thing is

that it is sharp. Maybe we are trying too hard to get it to look like the points the hunters make."

"Bah!" Yaiya dropped his tools and Shutok thought he might leave. Even as short-tempered as Yaiya was, Shutok wanted him to stay.

Shutok studied his work. This obsidian, like a living thing, had a stubborn personality of its own. He wondered if that was the reason the hunters forbad anyone else to make weapons or tools. Perhaps one had to know the secrets of the way before he could make spear points. Shutok knew that what he and Yaiya were doing was disrespectful. He expected to be punished for it, but he was intrigued by the craft. It was fun to be making something.

He held the stone in the palm of his left hand, the working edge of the point cushioned against the fleshy part of his thumb. With his right hand he tapped a stick along this edge, chipping off small flakes the size of fish scales. For smaller chipping, he held the pointed end of his stick against the edge of the rock and pushed hard, until a tiny flake came away.

But he did not know how to make it taper smoothly from the tip, how to make it less bulky in the middle, or how to make the notches for fastening it to a wooden shaft. Whenever he tried to do these things the obsidian broke in bigger chunks than he wanted. He decided to stop for the afternoon, afraid to get carried away and ruin the whole thing with one wrong blow.

"There," he said, satisfied with himself. It was ugly

compared to Aar's work, but it was probably sharp enough to cut already.

"What does it look like?" Yaiya asked. He had been brooding on top of his boulder, staring through the trees at the creek so raptly that Shutok knew he was not seeing anything — daydreaming about the killer of men, Shutok thought. Yaiya would not be content with becoming a hunter in the usual way. Now that he had hit upon this idea he would find it boring to sit alone for three days with nothing to eat and with only a fire for protection, waiting for a sign.

The sign might come from anything — the sky, an animal, the earth, the four winds. Whatever gave him this sign would become the source of his power, the medicine that made him a hunter. But Yaiya had *picked* the source of his power. If he had his way it would come from the killer of men and nothing else.

He turned Shutok's point over in his hand. "Not bad for a first try," he said, as if he had made many of them himself. "But to kill the sharp-toothed one I will need a better point than this one. Mine will have notches here so that it will not pull away from the shaft. The shaft will slow the wounded animal so that it will be easier to follow." He handed the point back to Shutok and returned to work on his own piece of obsidian.

Shutok looked at the stone in his hand as if it, and not Yaiya's criticism of it, were the reason for the resentment he was feeling. But then almost at once he felt guilty. He knew that Yaiya had not meant to offend him. His brother had often said worse things to him — cruel things — and he had not felt like this. Shutok realized with shame that he was jealous.

Instantly he buried his point in the sand, as though by doing so he could bury his jealousy, and marked the spot with the pointed stick that he had used for chipping. He had hardly smoothed the sand with his hands when Yaiya made a sound of frustration in his throat.

"What is the matter now?" Shutok asked.

"Stupid thing!" Yaiya picked up a rock that was beside him. Shutok watched coldly while his brother smashed his piece of obsidian to bits with it, cutting his hand on the sharp fragments.

Yaiya stormed off through the trees without another word, and Shutok was happy at first that he was gone. It was only a very short while before his loneliness closed in on him again, like the sand that he had smoothed over his hidden spear point.

Some of the leaves here and there along the creek had begun to change to their fall colors by the time Yaiya was finally told that he could go on his power journey. Even then, it was Ala, in her indirect way, who suggested to the hunters that he be allowed to make his quest.

"It grows cold at night, eh Mato?" she said one morning before the hunters left the cave. "And soon there will be another mouth to feed. Let us hope that you will bring us another boy, for we will need more hunters in the hungry times to come."

Mato held her hands on her swollen belly, her eyes cast down. She knew, just as everyone did, that Ala was not talking about her baby.

"There is enough to eat."

That was Aar's answer. He had said no, Yaiya was not ready, and they did not need his help. Could he know about the obsidian?

Shutok looked over at his brother. Yaiya's eyes begged Ala to say more, but Shutok wanted Aar's answer to stay the same.

"That is good," Ala said. "You would not want to go without food on a night colder than this one was, would you, Mato?" Mato looked scared and did not reply. Ala was clearly talking about Yaiya, for he would not eat anything during the three days that he would be gone.

Shutok expected Aar to punish Ala for her disrespect, but instead he turned to look into the eyes of Gan and Hnit. They talked it over among themselves without saying a word or moving a muscle.

"Prepare yourself," Aar said then, turning to look Yaiya sternly in the face. Somehow he *did* know about the obsidian, and Yaiya shriveled. "You will go tomorrow. Do not break the way again or you will find nothing—no sign, no power."

There was another look, this time directed at Shutok. He let his breath out with a long sigh of relief when the hunters left the cave.

Shutok took Aar's warning seriously. He had not stopped working on his point after Yaiya had destroyed his. Because he had been patient, doing only a little each day, Shutok felt that he had succeeded in making something useful, if not pretty. It had a tip so sharp and thin that he could almost see through it. And if the barbs were not the same shape on both sides, at least he was sure they would hold the point solidly into whatever prey he hunted with it. He left a short peg of stone between the barbs for fastening it onto a spear shaft. It was too bad he would never get to use it, he thought. He was going to hate having to break it up.

He crossed the creek only to find that someone had been to the clearing ahead of him. It could only have been Yaiya. Who else would have known just exactly where to look? When Shutok dug underneath the spot marked by the stick, his spear point was not there.

Yaiya stayed away from camp all afternoon, but when he returned to the cave that evening, Shutok was waiting for him. He had forgotten about breaking the point into pieces just as soon as he knew Yaiya had it.

"Come outside," he whispered. "I want to talk to you."

"Not now."

"Give it back to me, then. It isn't yours and I want it back."

"What, are you crazy?" Yaiya hissed at him, looking nervously at the others. They were listening now. "All right. Come on, then."

"I need it," Yaiya said when they were away from the cave.

"Don't you ever listen to what you are told?" Shutok lectured. "You are going to take a weapon, even after what Aar said this morning. I can't believe it. And besides, it doesn't belong to you. I made it and it's mine!"

"The hunters only say those things because they want to keep all the fun for themselves. And I will give it back to you."

"Give it to me now."

"I can't. I'll give it back when I return. Then you will be glad that you let me use it."

"You are not ready to go," Shutok burst out bitterly. "You have no respect for the way and I hope there is no sign. You are only a selfish boy, Yaiya, not a hunter!"

"And who are you to say that I am not ready? You should have died on the prairie. Or when the girl was hitting you like a dog at the river. If I have bad luck it will be because you did not die then and you have cursed me like this. You are full of evil, Shutok!"

Shutok had no reply for this, and as usual Yaiya had the last word. In the morning he did not go outside until he was sure that his brother was already away from camp.

The day was different with Yaiya gone, but not because Shutok missed his brother or worried about him. He gathered firewood as he always did, but he talked to an imaginary Yaiya instead of the pain that was his real companion. Now that it was too late, Shutok was able to think up stinging answers to Yaiya's last words to him, and he did not tire of repeating them all day long.

"You are the one who deserves this evil," he said. "I did not break the way — not as much as you did — but it crawled into me by mistake." Every time he echoed himself it seemed to improve, until by the end of the day he was able to fix the imaginary Yaiya with just a superior look and the words, "We will see. Just wait. We will see who is ready to become a hunter, you or me." And then, in his daydream, Shutok threw aside the crutch and walked away, cured, leaving his brother dumbfounded.

The second day Yaiya was gone, Shutok did not scold so much as reason. "Listen," he said, dragging his branches up the hill. "Do you really think you are a better hunter than Aar or Gan or Hnit? Men do not hunt the killers, so why do you think that a boy like you can do any better?" Then his reverie ended.

"Are you so lonely without Yaiya that you talk to yourself?" Shutok was furious that Ala and Uita had overheard him. The girl giggled and he felt his face burning.

"Bring a lot of wood," Ala said, smiling. "There will be celebrating tomorrow when Yaiya returns. All of us are going to the place where the creek enters the marsh. Maybe we can find something special to eat for our feast."

"Bring a lot of wood!" he muttered when they left, laughing at him as they went. "There is plenty of wood here already. See if I get more today! If you only knew what I know, Ala, maybe there would not be so much celebrating."

Shutok lay in the open, letting the heat soak into his body. The afternoon was warm, not hot, another warning that the season was changing. Soon it would be fall.

This was not the first time that he had given some thought to the season that was approaching. But there was nothing new to think about. He planned to follow the others when they left the marsh, that was all. Staying here meant giving up. His people were hunters and they did not store food for winter. Instead they traveled wherever the food was. That was the way, and Shutok had no idea how he would prepare for staying.

No, he decided, he would have to walk over the plains again. He might as well enjoy this chance to rest. He closed his eyes to nap, but he was not quite asleep when he heard someone back in camp.

Shutok sat up with a sigh. Out of the corner of his eye he saw movement, but when he looked he saw no one and he was puzzled. What had moved? Perhaps it was just ...

Then he saw it and froze. He had to look carefully to make out the shape of the cat. The rimrock was reflecting the bright sunlight into the boy's eyes. This was not a tawny-coated cougar, but something he had never seen before. It had spots, and they hid the animal so well, right there in the open, that Shutok was terrified to see how close it was. The spotted one stood still in the way that a deep river is held between its banks, the whole animal fluid and powerful but fixed.

Shutok felt the animal turning him inside out with its stare, but once looking into those yellow eyes there was no looking away. It seemed not to be looking at him, but through him, like clear water that one sees but looks beneath. At that moment it was not so much fear that Shutok felt, but power surging through his mind, churning up the bottom and turning over stones in the very deepest parts of his body. When the cat finally looked away, Shutok felt as if he had suddenly and rudely been jerked awake in the middle of an important dream.

53

Before it disappeared around the corner of the rimrock, the spotted one sniffed at the woodpile and the cold outdoor firepit. It went to the mouth of the cave and looked in. Then it was gone.

Shutok waited for the women to return from the marsh the way one waits for daylight during a night of close, frightful sounds — without moving a muscle.

It was only later, when he was describing the cat to Ala, that Shutok knew he had also seen — besides the penetrating eyes — the spots that were not really spots but rings like black and brown blossoms against the tan coat, the small ears, broad nose, the heavy chest.

"I have never seen such a one myself," she said when he had told her as much as he could remember. "But I have heard it called..." She paused because it was dangerous to speak the name of a man-killer. She whispered it. "Jaguar it is called. The people who live in the desert where we spend the winter speak of this animal. Of all the hunters of men, this one is the fiercest."

"This is the one of the cave," Mato said, bending over the cat's tracks. "Look. No other man-killer leaves pawprints as big as these." She began smoothing them out with her feet. "Perhaps it will not be able to follow its tracks back to us," she explained, but she could not have believed in her own trick. She was smoothing out the tracks because as long as they were there they frightened her.

That night and the next morning Ala's face wore a look of concern. She was worried that the cat would find Yaiya. She did not know that Yaiya was hunting the cat. But seeing the animal had put Shutok more at ease about his brother's safety. It meant that Yaiya was probably hunting in the wrong place.

The day drew on and it was an awkward wait. Had it been as hard, Shutok wondered, for Ala to wait night after night for him to stagger into their camps on the prairie? When Yaiya did not come and did not come, Shutok thought he understood why his mother had been impatient with him. It had been her struggle too. The constant uncertainty must have been worse than grief for Ala. But at least after waiting so many times for him, he thought that waiting for Yaiya must be easier for her. Or did it ever get easier?

The weather had a gloomy effect on them all. The sky was overcast, threatening rain, and a blustery wind blew Shutok's hair into his eyes and mouth. It was cold, and he felt better if he kept the fire blazing brightly. They waited, the hunters watching out over the marsh from the high rock that was their private place, the others restless around the camp, and Shutok poking at the fire.

"I will go get more wood," Shutok said to Ala. It was getting close to dark, and from the way his mother looked at him the boy could tell that she knew he wanted to try to find Yaiya. It was forbidden to go looking for someone when they were gone on their power journey, but she said it was all right for him to get more firewood.

"Uita, you go with Shutok to help. And don't go far."

For once he did not argue about the girl. They went down the trail, turned left at the creek, and walked toward the marsh. Uita followed closely behind Shutok. Whenever she walked with him she was too helpful, as if he needed careful watching to prevent him from hurting himself.

It sent a shock through Shutok when he saw his brother lying in the creek. He immediately feared the worst and he called out his brother's name with a trembling in his voice.

"Go away," Yaiya answered dully.

Shutok relaxed. "What are you doing there? We have been waiting all afternoon for you." Yaiya seemed to be taking a bath. They stepped closer.

"Is something the matter?"

"Phew!" the girl said, standing beside Shutok. Then he noticed it too, and he elbowed the girl to keep her quiet.

"Go away!" Yaiya said desperately, turning his head to look hopelessly at them. There were tears in his eyes and Shutok's heart went out to his brother. What a terrible thing to happen to him on his power journey!

"Where is my spear point?" Shutok asked.

"I threw it at the skunk and then it sprayed me. I did not go back after it."

"Come on. We will walk with you to the cave. Let me tell you what I saw in camp yesterday."

6

"WE MUST GO soon now," Shutok said to himself, rubbing his hands together to take the chill off them. When all the leaves were gold and red and brown it was time for them to pack their burden bundles and walk around the marsh to the prairie. That time had passed. They were waiting for Mato now. It seemed that they were always waiting for someone.

Ala kept promising the hunters, "She will need only a day or two more." Because it was Aar's young that Mato carried they agreed to the delay. It had been more days than anyone could count since the first frost and Mato's pains had not started yet. Ala was beginning to hint that something might be wrong.

The decision to leave would have to be made before long — maybe this afternoon — and Shutok wanted to be there when they finally made up their minds to go. He rubbed his hands together until they burned. Then he lifted his firewood again and carried it the rest of the way to camp. There was no woodpile outside any more. He set the wood inside the cave next to the firepit.

Mato was up. She walked cautiously, as if walking were

something she had not done for a long time. With her arms out for balance in the smoky, dark cave she looked like a standing bear. But she could walk. Other women had their children on the trek across the plains, so why couldn't Mato? Shutok wanted to leave right away, while there was someone other than him to slow everyone down.

A hide had been hung between two poles to cover the mouth of the cave. Daylight leaked in around the edges, but the cave was dreary by firelight and the smoke made Shutok's eyes water. He had just grown accustomed to the darkness when the hunters brushed aside the doorflap and entered in a dazzle of light. The boy moved out of their way. This was it, he thought. Everyone was here but the girl. She was gathering firewood.

"Scoot over, boy," Yaiya ordered. He thought he was being funny. Shutok moved farther out of the way. He had to sit with his back bent and his neck bowed under the low ceiling.

It had not taken Yaiya long to get over the humiliation of the skunk. That was partly Shutok's fault. If he had waited to tell his brother about seeing the spotted one — instead of blurting it out while he sat there in the stream — Yaiya would not have had time to invent a yarn about seeing it himself. By the time Yaiya came into camp, still reeking of skunk, he had his story ready. The hunters accepted it as true, but they probably knew better than to believe it now. The story grew and changed with every telling. And besides, Shutok knew that anyone who had power from the great killer could not act so small.

"We must go now or we will not catch the herds," Aar

said. Mato looked ashamed of herself, as if the delay were all her fault. It had been Ala's idea to wait here until Mato had given birth, and it was Ala who answered the hunter.

"You have some evil, Mato. It should have come by now, don't you think?" Mato nodded. "If we go now there may be trouble." Mato nodded again. Shutok wondered how they could tell, but Aar did not ask for an explanation.

"Are you getting lazy, Ala, or too old? Perhaps you would like to stay here." The air was full of tension, and Ala was quiet. She put another piece of wood on the fire before she said anything.

"I am afraid for you, Mato," she said at last. She was careful not to talk directly to Aar. "It is some magic, and only magic can make it right." The fresh stick burned brightly, but only coals were left of it before anyone said anything else. The silence was thick like smoke.

It was Gan who spoke at last. This was Shutok's father, an unsmiling man whose voice was strange to the boy because he spoke so seldom. His teeth were black and broken, and everyone knew that the scowl he always had on his face was due to the pain in his mouth. He was always sucking his teeth, his forehead knotted, a waspish look in his eyes.

"The people of the marsh would have a shaman," he said. He was not supporting Ala against Aar. He was only stating a fact.

"What would we pay the shaman?" Aar asked. There was respect in his voice, for he valued Gan's advice.

"There is the girl," he replied. Ala looked alarmed and

Shutok was impatient to hear what she would say about Gan's suggestion. She took enough time to think about it carefully.

"For the girl we should get more," she said, but to Shutok it seemed like a fair trade, one life for another.

"Yes," Aar agreed. "We will ask him to make a hunting charm for us as well."

"And Shutok," Ala said. The boy's head hit the stone roof when she said his name. "Don't you think that the magic of a shaman could remove the evil from him too?" She had asked Mato again. Yaiya answered.

"By some trick? By hiding stones in his mouth and then pretending to suck them out of Shutok's back?" His tone was insulting, but Ala could no longer tell him to be quiet. He was a hunter. Aar let him know that his comments were not welcome by ignoring him.

"We will drive a hard bargain for the girl," he said, standing to end the council.

It was cold when the hunters left in the morning for the marsh and the day did not seem to get any warmer as it wore on. The sun was dull behind a thin layer of clouds that covered the sky everywhere, making it a good day to stay near the fire. When Shutok came across the girl sitting by herself he knew that she was taking it hard and that she wanted to be alone. She was singing the same song he had heard first at the river. It seemed to be the only song she knew. He listened to her for a while before deciding to speak to her. It was a good song and she sang it often, sometimes happily, sometimes sadly. Today it sounded like a death song.

"Why are you so unhappy?" he asked. "There is much to be happy about. If the shaman comes, he will help Mato and the hunters and me," he explained excitedly. A cure! Every time he thought about it his heart jumped inside his chest. But he was not being selfish. "You should be pleased that you are worth so much in trade," he added.

"Uita likes Shutok's people," was all she said. When she looked at him with tears in her eyes they looked even more crooked than they usually did. Shutok told himself that he was not going to feel sorry for her. He went on down the creek in search of wood, but the sharp edge of his excitement had been dulled.

The shaman was a tall, richly dressed man who was not old. Shutok thought he might have lived as many seasons as Hnit, the youngest of the hunters except for Yaiya. He wore his wealth where everyone could see it: many strings of shells and bone beads, a medicine pouch decorated with more beads and with porcupine quills, all of this over a fine, warm robe of twisted bird skins and feathers.

Shutok had never seen so many beautiful and valuable things, but the most striking thing about the shaman was not how tall he was or how rich. He was dirty — remarkably dirty. There were stains of greasy paint on his face and arms, as if he never washed it off. His hair was matted with filth and it hung loose around his shoulders in a hopeless tangle.

Shutok gaped at the man, not knowing quite what to think. His shocking appearance was a sure sign of powerful magic, and that magic was his last hope of ever becoming a hunter like Yaiya. But it filled the boy with panic to think that the magic might not take. He could not bear to have something go wrong. He stayed away from the circle of people standing just outside the cave, watching everything nervously.

Ala and Mato brought food from inside, but the shaman said he wanted to see the girl first. He talked in the sign language of the plains, but his face said more than his hands. Now that he saw what manner of people he had come to help, he did not trust them and he did not hide his scorn. Shutok's people were so poor that before he even decided to eat with them he wanted to see his payment.

Aar led Uita to the shaman and left her looking terrified in front of him. She started to go back to Ala but before she could take two steps the man grabbed her by the hair and threw her to the ground. She lay cringing at his feet while he walked around her, kicking her a couple of times the way a hunter kicks a bison to make sure it is dead. As he looked down on her, Shutok thought the shaman's face had the gray, stony look of someone used to hurting others. And not out of anger, the way Shutok had once wanted to hurt Uita. The shaman seemed to be enjoying it for no good reason.

"What do you want in exchange for her?" he signed.

Aar pointed to Mato. "We want a charm for the birth of her young and another for good hunting on our journey. We will leave as soon as the young is born."

The shaman signaled his agreement with a nod and

Shutok heard an involuntary groan escape from his own throat. Were they going to forget about him?

Ala now held her hand up, palm open at her shoulders, and moved it back and forth to indicate that there was something more to be talked about. The look in Aar's eyes would have driven anyone else back, but Ala stepped boldly before the shaman.

"We want you to drive the evil from my son." She called to Shutok who lifted himself from the ground with the stick that Uita had given him. He had not realized he was so cold; when he started to walk toward the center of the group he was shivering so hard that he could barely control his steps. Peering into the man's face to see if he could tell what his answer would be, the boy wished that he had not looked.

When their eyes met it was like water meeting fire. Shutok had no control over his eyes and he was unable to return the man's stare. He remembered looking into the eyes of the spotted one and having no control over his eyes then, either, but this was much more awful. There was no mistaking the shaman's answer. He refused.

Aar did not seem to care. Shutok knew that he would not bicker with the shaman, because Ala had insulted him. She should not have spoken up like that.

The hunter offered again to trade Uita for a hunting charm and for the birth of Mato's young. The shaman nodded in agreement. He pulled a stone pipe from his medicine pouch. The two of them were ready to smoke, sealing the agreement, when Ala stopped them.

"This is not the trade we agreed upon yesterday," she

63

said, talking to Aar as if he were not a hunter. She had gone too far this time, showing disrespect for him in front of this important stranger. Aar hit her on the side of the face before she had a chance to say anything more.

There would be no charm for Shutok. He felt such relief just getting out from under the shaman's evil eyes that his disappointment was slow to sink in. Later, after the others had gone inside, Shutok asked Ala, "Why did he refuse?"

"He was afraid," she answered. One hand covered the side of her face. When she took it away Shutok could see the bruise where Aar had hit her.

"I don't understand. What was there to be afraid of?"

"He knew that his medicine was not strong enough. The evil in your back is more powerful than his magic." Ala's voice sounded distant, but there was scorn for the shaman in what she said. "He was afraid to lose face. And he might have been afraid of us, too. Among our people, what goes for the sick man also goes for the shaman. That is the way. If the sick man gets better, then the shaman is paid his price. But if the shaman makes magic that kills the sick man, then it follows that the shaman should die. This one did not want to risk it."

"But then he is only a coward."

Ala did not answer, but Shutok knew by her silence that she agreed. He decided that this dirty, rich man was his enemy. He felt cheated, but there was nothing he could do to cheat the shaman in return.

Uita pushed aside the doorflap and stepped out. Even in the half-light of evening it was obvious that something was very wrong. Her face had the look of someone wading into dark, uncertain water.

"What is it, child?" Shutok envied the tenderness that was in his mother's voice when she talked to Uita.

"He sends Uita to the marsh now, to get reeds," the girl answered. It was the time of day when the sky was gray right down to the ground and every bush and boulder looked like it might be something dangerous. It would be pitch black by the time she got to the marsh.

"Let us go together," Ala said, getting to her feet. A look of relief spread across the girl's face.

Uita and Ala left for the marsh, running while there was still some light to see by, and Shutok went inside.

The shaman was making paint by grinding lumps of hard clay into powder on a flat stone. The clay was red and yellow. He must have carried the ochre with him, because Shutok knew of no place near their camp where the colored dirt could be found. When the shaman had ground the clay into two piles of red and yellow dust he mixed grease into it. Then he began to paint his face and arms, singing now as he smoothed the oily colors onto his dirty skin with his fingers.

The song was not a pleasing one. All songs were sung in a sharp part of the voice that was not used for talking, but this song did not stay there. Instead of holding to two or three pitches it jumped all around in the shaman's throat. It was hard to listen to because it never went where Shutok expected it to go. It would be nearly impossible to learn.

But, he thought, who would want to learn it? It was

too ugly. He did not know what it said, but it sounded as if there were not many words to it. It was mostly noise.

The shaman painted his face red and then carefully drew red and yellow lines down his arms from his shoulders to his fingertips. He finished and began to dance, still wearing his robe of bird skins, which he spread open and closed like wings. His neck was bent and he stepped around the floor as if he worried about tripping over someone or bumping his head on the ceiling. Shutok thought the dance was as ugly as the song, but it was supposed to be that way. The shaman was driving evil spirits from the cave.

Shutok turned his eyes away from the demon that seemed to rise out of the flames in front of him. He looked at the doorway. Ala and Uita had been gone long enough. He heard something outside, but when no one pushed aside the doorflap he thought it must have been his imagination. How could he hear anything over the noise the shaman was making? It was so close inside the cave that it sounded as though he was singing inside the boy's head.

Tuta was more interesting to watch than the shaman. He had his hands over his eyes but he was peeking out through his fingers. If the shaman stepped close to him he buried his face in Mato's lap. He was not the only one who looked scared.

Aar stared into the fire. The other hunters warily turned their heads to watch the dancing figure wherever it went, but he seemed to be listening to something else. It had been a long trip around the marsh to the shaman's village, and then nearly all the villagers disappeared into the marsh before he could make them understand what he wanted. Perhaps he was tired, Shutok thought. The other three hunters might have been tired, too, but their eyes could not leave the nightmare of the shaman.

The song ended so abruptly that Shutok gasped and looked to see what had happened. Everyone's eyes were wide, even Aar's, but the shaman simply sat down. The song was over, that was all. Shutok shook his head in disbelief. How anyone could tell when the end of that song was coming was a puzzle to him. The sudden silence set him more on edge than the song had.

Aar got up and pushed open the door. He looked out for a long time. The night looked very black from where Shutok sat. He remembered to worry about Ala and Uita. No one spoke after Aar came back to his place beside the fire. Only the shaman seemed comfortable in the silence he had created.

When Uita returned she was just there in the doorway without a sound to let them know she was coming. Mato screamed and Shutok jumped half out of his skin. The firelight reflecting white off Uita's face made it seem that only her head was there. Then Ala stepped up behind her, breathing hard, and the shaman's spell of silence was broken. Everyone laughed nervously — everyone but the shaman.

He began to sing again after taking the reeds from Uita. This was a song that made more sense to Shutok, although he still could not understand the words. It was like the songs his own people sang to bring courage and determination to the hunters.

The reeds were supple because they were fresh. The shaman worked them without wetting them. He bent some, tied them in place with others, and produced a charm that looked like a bison. It was as large as his hand. He made others, using almost all the reeds, and the hunters were pleased. He put the charms on ledges and in pockets in the darkest parts of the cave. Then this song ended.

The shaman made one more charm while the hunters made their places ready for sleeping beside the fire. This charm looked like a man, and he gave it to Mato.

"Tomorrow," he signed to her, and Mato nodded her head in understanding.

Uita settled in her usual place next to Ala. She was already asleep, one arm thrown over her eyes and her mouth open, when the shaman stepped carefully through the bodies of the hunters and kicked her.

Shutok sat up at the same time Uita did, feeling as confused as she looked. A new excitement sliced through the boy, but as sharply as he felt it he could not understand it. It was hatred and something else all jumbled up together. He tried to focus on the hatred, but the other kept coming into his mind like a mixed-up dream where all the faces run together. The shaman and Uita — what was it?

The shaman pointed but Uita did not know what he wanted. Ala told her.

"Go with him, child. You are his now. Rich men have slaves to keep them warm at night."

Uita lay with her back to the man. When she saw Shutok watching, she made a face and pinched her nose to let him know that the dirty shaman stunk. Shutok angrily rolled onto his other side. He did not sleep well. It was the coldest night yet.

SHUTOK WOKE EARLY because he was cold. Ala was up before him, poking at the coals to get the fire started. She was raising cold-smelling ash that clouded the air. He could see specks of it caught in the rays of daylight that thrust in around the edges of the door.

"If you are cold go get firewood. Small pieces. I wish we could burn the wood from this nest," Ala said, not lowering her voice for the sake of the sleepers. "Brrr! This has to be winter. Go get wood, will you?"

Shutok raised himself unsteadily and put his crutch under his arm. The pain in his back was always worse after the cold of the night.

"At least *he* slept warm," Ala added bitterly, speaking softly this time. Shutok looked at the shaman, sleeping with one arm over Uita's shoulder. She was rolled up in a ball, her knees pulled up under her chin.

The sunrise made Shutok stop at the mouth of the cave. It was a sunrise that could mean bad weather ahead — blood red on the horizon and the color of salmon flesh higher up where the clouds were broken. They might be leaving the cave just in time to be caught by the first storm of winter.

Shutok looked down before stepping out. What he saw on the ground made him turn back.

"Ala..."

"What is it?" she asked.

"Come look." In the unfrozen sand at the mouth of the cave were the four-toed tracks of the spotted one. Ala woke the hunters. She was careful not to let anyone walk over the ground where the tracks were until Aar could study them.

"So, that one again!" he said.

"And look here." Hnit pointed to one of the pawprints that had been stepped on by someone walking into the cave. Shutok wondered how that could have happened. No one had gone out yet this morning, and he thought he would have known if someone had stepped outside in the middle of the night.

"The girl," Aar said. "The killer must have been here last night just before Ala and Uita returned from the marsh. They walked right where the cat had been, and they did not even know it. They were both lucky."

Shutok remembered that Aar had gone to the doorflap to look outside after the shaman had finished his first song. Perhaps the spotted one had been there then, and maybe Aar had frightened it away.

"It wants this place back now that it is getting cold outside," Ala said to Mato. "The shaman's magic had better work. We have to leave here before this killer catches one of us."

But no one had to tell the shaman to hurry. He looked at those tracks and then seemed to be in a hurry of his own. He knew exactly what had made them. Even before Shutok went to get the firewood that Ala had asked for, the shaman began to make magic for Mato. He ground up herbs that he had carried wrapped in a leaf inside his medicine pouch. Then he mixed the herbs into water and gave the potion to Mato to drink.

Shutok stayed inside as long as he could. Nothing happened to Mato.

"Shutok! What are you doing in here still?"

"I am going. Small pieces?"

Big pieces or small, Shutok could not fetch wood faster than the shaman burned it. Uita was sent to help him and after that he was able to spend more time inside, but he still did not get to see much of the shaman's magic. Then in the afternoon Mato's pains began.

They were easy at first. Sometimes Mato smiled when the pains came, but her teeth were clenched tight. Once when Shutok was in the cave he heard her praise the shaman.

"This is comfort, eh Ala? Here in the shelter of the cave and with this big fire for warmth. Not like on the prairie. Do you remember what a time it was with Tuta? This shaman with his fancy clothes is a person of great power."

When the sun fell, Shutok knew that he and Uita had not brought enough wood to last through the night. It was so cold inside the cave that the boy could see his breath.

The shaman piled wood on recklessly. Unless he burned a little at a time he would run out. Shutok thought there would be frost all the way inside the cave by morning unless he conserved fuel.

Mato was complaining by the time they went to their sleeping places. Ala kept Tuta with her, trying to comfort him, but when his mother cried out he was a sorry sight.

"It was like this when you were born," Ala said to him, stroking his head. "Except that we were out in the open then, a long way from here. The pains started in the morning and you did not come until late in the afternoon. I carried you into camp myself. A hard one you were, Tuta. Mato will be all right. Try to sleep."

Some time later the shaman began to sing his song for driving away evil. Shutok rested fitfully. Mato's pain and that awful song were like a nightmare that stayed the same whether he was awake or asleep. He was asleep when the shaman kicked him.

The boy looked up, blinking and confused. It was not morning. He was too dazed to dodge and the shaman kicked him again, hard. "Tell him to stop it. Why is he kicking me?" he yelled. Then Shutok saw that the others were looking on. He knew they were not going to help him but he did not know why. "What is wrong?" he pleaded.

Mato began screaming and Shutok was ashamed that he had been able to sleep through the agony that filled the cave.

"Get out," Aar shouted. The shaman's foot was aimed

at Shutok again. He grabbed his stick and threatened to strike back.

"You have given your evil to Mato — maybe to the rest of us," the hunter growled, standing beside the shaman. His face was pinched with fury. Shutok could not escape without turning his back to the two men. He sat there helplessly, brandishing his stick awkwardly until Aar grabbed it out of his hands.

"If Mato dies . . . if Mato dies I will kill you!" Aar spat at him. Shutok crawled from the cave with the shaman kicking him in the backside until he was out the doorway.

The air outside was icy cold and the frosty ground bit into the boy's hands and knees. Shutok knew that he had to keep moving or he would freeze to death before morning. He crawled back and forth in front of the cave, thinking about what this meant. Ala had warned him as long ago as the river that he could be blamed for anything that might go wrong. He had no doubts that Aar would carry out his threat if the worst happened to Mato.

But Shutok also remembered what Ala had told him about the shaman paying with his life if his patient died. Shutok thought that he was being used. He got all the blame, and the shaman was not getting any. Shutok hated the shaman, and thinking about getting even almost seemed to be keeping him warmer.

He heard Mato intermittently until morning, holding his breath every time she fell silent. He listened for Aar's footsteps. It was always a relief to hear Mato again.

The sun gave Shutok light to see by, but no warmth. He went down the path to the creek, still on his hands and knees. Aar had probably burned his crutch when the wood ran out, he thought.

The water had ice on it, and he realized with a shudder that the only way to get where he was going was to crawl through it. Shutok promised himself a huge fire when he got to the little clearing where he and Yaiya had worked together on their pieces of obsidian. He would build a fire big enough to singe his hair and make his skin red like the summer sun.

The sharpened stick he had made his spear point with was just where he had left it. Shutok had not been to the clearing since the day Yaiya had gone on his power journey. With the leaves gone from the trees it did not seem so private, but he wanted to be where he could watch the others.

Shutok had seen fire made so often that he knew exactly what to do. He found dry grass for tinder and wrapped it tightly around the sharp end of his hard chipping stick. Resting this end on a piece of softer wood, he twirled the stick in his hands until the grass smoldered, then lighted. But the boy settled for less than a bonfire. Since he had to crawl, he could barely gather enough wood to keep a small fire burning.

About midday Shutok saw the hunters leave the cave. Ala came down to the creek once, filled her waterskin, and went back. She had to know where he was, but she did not look up. Uita was out and around too, gathering firewood. Shutok wanted to know about Mato. Whatever was happening, it was obvious that he was being blamed for it.

It was late in the day when Uita walked into Shutok's camp. She startled him, sneaking up from behind him with quiet, quick steps.

"Oh, it's you!" he said. "Why did you sneak up behind me like that?"

"So no one will see," she said. She stood with one of the boulders between her and the creek so that she would be out of sight if anyone happened to look.

"Mato?" he asked at once. She looked away and began to cry.

"Then why did you come here?" he asked angrily, beginning to cry himself. Mato, with her gentle common sense, was his friend and a kinswoman. "It's true. I am so full of evil that I am a danger to everyone. It is against the way for me to live any longer."

"Mato is not dead," she corrected him. "She has eaten something and now she is asleep."

"Why are you crying, then? You bring me good news. Did you come to get me?" he asked, forgetting that she had come secretly into his camp.

"The young did not live," she answered. "The shaman says it is Shutok's fault and he told the men to kill you. That is why I came, to tell you. Now Shutok will run and hide."

"What good would that do? I could not get far without my crutch, so they would find me anyway."

"Aar burned the stick. He said it was bad magic, against the way, and that I was bad to give it to you."

"They will just leave me here, and this time I will not be able to follow them."

"Uita wants to stay too. I will not go with the bad man."

"And starve to death? But he will not let you stay."

Uita stood looking into Shutok's fire, and he thought he knew what she was thinking. Then she looked up at him with what looked like hatred in her face, and he knew that he was wrong. She had been waiting for him to say something, but he did not know what it was. Without a word, she ran from his camp, going the way she had come.

"Good-bye, Uita," he called after her.

Shutok was hungry but he had nothing to eat. He gathered firewood until it was too dark and then curled up close to his little fire and tried to sleep.

A gust of wind made the boy wish he had built the fire against one of the boulders instead of in the middle of the clearing. He sat up with that thought, but it was too late to move now. He shuddered. It was the wind again, rattling the dry leaves and whipping the flames in front of him. The white tree trunks seemed to walk in the flickering light, and above him the empty branches sighed and bent and seemed to reach down for him. Shutok lay down again and shut his eyes, knowing that he had to go to sleep before he scared himself.

He woke uneasily from a dream he could not remember, and for a few horrible heartbeats he did not know where he was. He had grown so used to sleeping in the cave that he had forgotten what it was like to wake up each morning in a different place.

But it was not morning. The fire was still burning brightly, so he knew that he had not slept long. He put on more wood — too much wood — and went back to sleep.

Shutok came into the dream just where he had left it. There he was again, coming closer, dirt sticking to the paint on his face. The shaman had a spear pointed at Shutok's throat. The boy tried to move out of the way but he seemed not to have his crutch, and his legs, as if they were tied, refused to move.

Then the man's eyes changed color. They were yellow. The shaman was the killer of men and just as the spear touched his throat Shutok woke with a scream. When he was awake and he knew he was awake the yellow eyes were still staring at him and the spear was still sticking in his throat. Shutok whimpered and felt sick. Then he yelled.

"Ouch!" He sat up and scooted away from the fire. Coals had rolled out of it, one of them burning his throat. The cat's eyes were two others, not even the same size. Shutok looked around nervously. There was nothing there — nothing that he could see, anyway — but the terror that woke him was still with him. He threw rocks into the trees to scare away any animal that might be lurking there, but he stopped when he remembered what had happened to Yaiya. His brother had thrown his spear at something he could not see in the night, and it had turned out to be a skunk.

His presence of mind returned to him and he put more wood on the fire. This was just how a hunter on a power journey had to spend his nights, he reminded himself, and he was determined not to panic again. When the wood was burned he lay nearly in the embers of his fire, waiting for morning without shutting his eyes.

The shaman was the first to leave. It was hardly light, but from where he watched, Shutok could see the man's steamy breath and the red paint still on his face. The boy's blood surged and he looked away.

Uita followed him. She was so slow that the shaman stopped to wait for her. The man gave her a cuff on the ear.

Before the sun's bright edge reached Shutok's camp the others descended the trail to the creek and then walked down the little valley toward the marsh. The hunters led, carrying just their weapons. Although there was no smoke from Shutok's dead fire, the men knew that he was there watching them. Yaiya glanced once in Shutok's direction, but he looked back to the trail before letting his eyes meet Shutok's over the distance.

Ala was with Mato and Tuta. Something fell from her burden bundle when the three of them reached the creek, and Tuta started to pick it up. Shutok did not hear what Ala said, but Tuta straightened up before touching it and Mato looked up directly to Shutok. The boy felt guilt all over his face like the shaman's paint.

They went on.

"Wait!" The word filled his chest but got no farther than his throat. "Wait! I'm coming." The sunlight reached him and he did not move.

8

IT WAS ONLY a bird looking for bugs. Although he had just seen his family leave he took it for granted, when he heard it scratching through the leaves and looked up, that someone would be standing there. They were gone for good, he told himself. He would never see them again. Still, part of his mind could not accept that, and the bird disappointed him.

He crawled down to the creek and found the food that Ala had dropped for him. It had been nearly two days since he had eaten, and the meat barely filled him up. With no thought of saving any for the next day, Shutok ate it all before laboring up the trail to the cave.

The doorflap was still in place. Ala's grinding bowl had not been moved. In the dim light their footprints could be seen everywhere, and it seemed only as if the others had stepped out on an errand and that they would return soon.

But there was freshly turned dirt in one corner, and Shutok knew what was buried there. The reality of his solitude sank in with the thought that there would be no one around to bury him. His family would find his scattered bones when they returned to the cave in the spring.

Shutok felt the ashes in the firepit. They were still warm, so he knew that there were live coals underneath. He did not uncover them. First he had to go for wood.

He crawled to the entrance before he remembered the nest. There was enough wood there to burn for days and days. What difference could it make now if he broke the way?

"I will only need a little of it. You will not even notice that any of the wood is gone," he said aloud to the spirit of the nest-builder. He pulled away a few small sticks and waited. Nothing happened, so he took enough for a small fire.

Then he slept. When he woke up it was already dark. There was nothing to do but try to sleep some more. If only he could sleep until the end came, and not wake up once!

But it was not so easy to sleep again after sleeping most of the day. A time or two he opened his eyes expecting to see the others there in their sleeping places. Once, Ala's face was so clear that he thought she was going to speak to him. Then he woke up excitedly, only to find an empty, dark cave, and he knew that he had been dreaming again.

He closed his eyes and her face came to him once more. Being able to see her like this, when he was not asleep, was surely magic. Shutok listened for her voice, but the fire was all he heard. Then he was asleep and dreaming again. He knew he was asleep and he did not want to wake up.

In this dream the fire had gone out. There was little light, but when he lifted his head he saw Uita at the mouth of the cave.

"Shutok?" he heard. "Shutok?"

He looked at her without answering. He was afraid that he would wake up. The girl's face looked this way and that way as if trying to see him, and Shutok wondered if dream-spirits could not see in the dark.

"Shutok, are you there?" she said. The spirit walked inside, and the boy discovered that this was no dream. He sat up suddenly and began scooting away from her — it.

"Are you a ghost?" he asked.

"What? I am cold and tired. Where are you, Shutok?"

Shutok stayed in the darkest part of the cave, but he was beginning to think that this *was* Uita, not a spirit. She was putting wood on the fire. He wanted to stay hidden until he was sure about her, but she would be able to see him as soon as the wood caught.

"What are you doing here?" he asked, his voice trembling. Then the fire caught and he held his arm over his eyes in the sudden light.

"The shaman ran away," she said. "I came back." It was Uita! Shutok's caution gave way and he began talking as if he had not seen another person for many moons on end.

"The fire," he said. "We can build up the fire from the nest. Tell me again what happened. Why did the shaman run? There is nothing left to eat. Ala dropped some food for me, but I ate it all. Tomorrow we can . . ."

"I will rest now," she interrupted. She went to her

sleeping place — the place she had shared with Ala before the shaman came. Shutok built the fire up and lay watching the girl across it. He did not sleep again that night.

She was still sleeping when daylight poked in around the doorflap. "Come on, wake up," Shutok whispered. He wanted to talk. Watching her breathing so peacefully made him more and more impatient. He went to the nest and purposely pulled out a branch that upset several others. The noise when they fell to the ground woke her. She sighed and then rubbed her eyes.

"Sorry," he lied. "What did you say about the shaman running away? Will he be back for you?" Shutok had been thinking this over, and he had decided that they should try to hide from the shaman before he came.

"Nothing to eat?" she asked.

"Nothing," Shutok answered. He repeated his question, and added, "We must decide fast upon something to do. He could be here any time now."

"The shaman is gone. We ran by a stream on the other side of the marsh, a long way from here. We saw the spotted one on a branch over the trail. The shaman ran away, and the spotted one followed him."

"What happened to the shaman? Is he dead?"

"I think so. I did not look. After I ran away from there to hide I did not see the shaman again, so I think the spotted one ate him. Then there was nowhere else to go, so I came here to find you."

"But you do not know for sure what happened to him?"

"No. Maybe the spotted one took just one bite. Bad men must taste bad too!"

He laughed at her joke, but Shutok was worried. He remembered dreaming about the shaman and the spotted one. The boy was sure that Uita's story fit in somehow. Shutok put his hand to his throat and felt the place where the coal had burned him. He did not dare believe that the shaman was dead.

"What will we do now?" he asked.

"Find something to eat," she said.

Shutok watched her go, helpless without his crutch. She was gone all day. He waited uneasily, still half-expecting the shaman to come for her. When she stayed away so long, his fears grew and grew until he was angry. He scolded her when finally she did return.

"Where have you been all day?" he demanded.

"Hunting." Uita held up a small rabbit by its hind legs.

"You have been gone since morning just for that? How was I supposed to know if something had happened to you? What if the shaman had come back? I can't even walk without my stick. You better not do that again!"

"You want to starve, then?" She was angry too. It had not been easy to catch the rabbit.

"That is not much better than starving," Shutok argued, pointing at it.

"Then Shutok does not have to eat the rabbit. I will eat it!"

"That's fine with me!" he shouted. "No one asked you to come here anyway. And I think you ran away from the shaman. You just made up that story about the spotted one."

Uita did not answer him. She ate the rabbit while the

boy sulked across the fire from her. He had not eaten that day, but he would not ask her to share.

When she was finished eating, Uita went to her sleeping place and sang herself to sleep. It was the same song she always sang. Shutok was so angry with her for ignoring him that he picked up a piece of firewood and was about to hit her with it, before he remembered the riverbank. He put the stick in the fire and tried to sleep.

In the morning she left without a word, and he knew that she would stay away until dark just to annoy him. "Let her," he grumped. "And she is wrong if she thinks that I will be the first one to give in and talk." He went out to look for his own food.

The cold shocked him when he left the cave. Gray clouds that looked like huge flat rocks were low in the sky. Shutok thought about his family. They had far to go, and they had waited too long. It was going to snow.

By the end of the day Shutok was so hungry that he hoped Uita had forgotten their argument. He saw no game when he was outside, and he was amazed to see Uita come into the cave carrying another rabbit. Shutok was ashamed when he saw what else she had.

"Here," she said, holding out a forked stick like the one Aar had burned. Shutok's stomach growled as he reached to take it from her, and he blushed.

"Now at least I can help by gathering firewood," he said, hoping that that would do for "thank you."

Uita began skinning the rabbit for cooking. "May I help?" Shutok asked. The question brought a smile to her face, but Uita did not tease him about his pouting fit the night before. She handed the rabbit to Shutok and rested while he cooked their dinner.

"I think it will snow tonight," she said when they were eating. "We will not worry about the shaman now. Even if he ran away from the spotted one, he will not come in the snow."

"Hmm," Shutok agreed, chewing. "But what will we eat?"

"Rabbits do not sleep in winter," she said with a shrug.

When they had eaten, Shutok went through the bones again to make sure that they had wasted nothing. If they did not starve it would be a miracle, he thought.

From then on there was snow. It was not yet the dead of winter, but even on the warmest days the snow did not leave the shadows. Shutok gathered firewood and made several trips each day to the creek to keep a waterhole open in the ice.

But added to these chores was work that he resented. While Uita hunted, Shutok split the bones of the animals they ate to make needles, cured their hides, and with sinew for thread sewed clothing for himself and the girl.

"This is women's work," he grumbled. When Uita was there he was irritable and fault-finding. "It is not fair that you get to do all the hunting while I have to sit here all day," he complained.

Then one night she returned empty-handed and solemn. They had been together long enough for the moon to grow full from a sliver, and Shutok had made a habit of nagging spitefully about what a poor hunter Uita was.

As she sat down, catching her breath, Shutok said,

"What? Again nothing? And again hungry! I did *my* job. See? Wood enough to last until morning, and I finished your mittens. Some hunter you are. A girl!" He saw that he had made her cry and he was happy. That would teach her who the leader was!

Uita held her head in her hands. "The killer of men is outside," she said indistinctly. Shutok heard her but thought that he was mistaken. "The spotted one. The same one. He is here now," she explained.

"How do you know? Did you see its tracks?"

"I saw him. I had two rabbits. Big, fat ones. I thought, 'Shutok will be happy to see these. He will not call Uita names.' But at the creek I saw it. When I stopped to drink at the waterhole I looked up and saw it watching. I ran, and I left the rabbits so the spotted one would eat them and not me."

"Did it chase you?" Shutok asked, looking with alarm toward the doorflap.

"I did not look back. I just ran, like the time of the shaman. I thought, 'now the claws will pull me to the ground, now I will feel the teeth in my throat.' I will stay here now. I will not hunt alone again."

Shutok went to the entrance and peeked around the edge of the doorflap. Uita had just come in but already it was nearly dark outside. The nights were so long, he thought with dread. He did not see any sign of the animal.

"It will not make much difference whether we stay inside," he said, coming back to the fire. "The spotted one wants this cave for the winter. I do not know what we can do to keep it out."

"Keep the fire burning," she said.

"But what will happen after we burn all the wood in the nest?" he asked. "And we have no food. We will have to go outside sooner or later. No, we must think of something else."

Uita sang herself to sleep. Shutok lay awake wondering what to do. He went to sleep thinking he had a plan, but when he told Uita about it the next morning, his plan did not seem like much.

"The killer will be coming anyway," he said, pausing to look into her eyes. He had grown used to the way Uita's left eye wandered. It was the right one that looked back at him when he talked to her. "There is nothing we can do to keep it out of here. So I think we should not wait until we are too weak from hunger to do something."

"But where can we go? It snows."

"That is not what I mean," he said. "I think we should stay here, but we must be ready for the sharp-toothed one when it comes. Listen! We can take sticks from the nest and sharpen them in the fire. If we sit with our backs to the wall and point the stakes so that the killer will jab itself on them, then it cannot come close enough to hurt us. We can throw spears at it until it goes away. The only way it will leave us alone is if we hurt it."

"Crazy!" she exclaimed in dismay. "Shutok will feed Uita to this animal." She began to cry, but this time her tears made him angry.

"Then you think of something better!" he shouted. He went to the nest and began pulling sticks out of it. They had burned more of the nest than he had thought. In no time at all Shutok had it all pulled apart. The sticks that were long enough and straight enough to be made into spears he piled near the fire. The rest he pushed back into the corner, hoping that the nest-builder's spirit would not be as angry if he did not take it all.

"Well," he said, standing over Uita, "are you going to help me or not?"

"What do we do now?"

"We need to make a sharp end on each one of these sticks. Here, I will show you how to do it." Shutok held one of the dry sticks in the fire just until the end caught. Then he rubbed out the flames against a hearth stone. This was repeated until the stick had a sharp, fire-hardened point. "It is not as good as a stone point, but it is the best we can do."

They made more spears than Shutok could count on his hands. There were more sticks to sharpen, and Shutok said, "You keep making spears while I set the sharp ones in the floor."

He went to the deepest part of the cave, where he had decided that they would make their stand. He set the spears into the floor like stakes, the sharpened ends pointing out toward the center of the cave. When the corner was protected they took down the skin door.

"I do not like this," Uita said.

"But we have to make the killer come inside," Shutok explained once more. "If we do not make it go away it will just stay outside until we starve or until it catches one of us. We do not have any choice."

Shutok made two more good, long spears from the poles

that had held up the doorflap, while Uita warmed the hide by holding it up to the fire. When all was ready they spread the coals so the fire would go out. They threaded their way carefully through the stakes.

"Do not fall now," Uita cautioned.

They settled down to wait, wrapped in the stiff hide. It had taken them all day to get ready, and after the coals winked out everything was black. The heat did not last long. Shutok shuddered when the wind reached in, stole some of his warmth, and then came back more boldly. He held one of the spears he had made from the door poles. The blunt end of it was wedged firmly into a crack in the wall behind him. The room where he had spent so many nights seemed vast in such blackness. The boy's eyes were confused, with nowhere to focus. Beside him Uita began to sing her song.

SHUTOK NUDGED UITA as soon as daylight began to give
shape to things. "You watch now," he said. "I will sleep.
Wake me if you see anything — anything at all, no matter
how small." He shifted to a more comfortable position,
not letting his hand leave the spear that he had held all
night. Places that had been warm next to Uita were cold
after he moved, but he fell asleep quickly. Then, all too
soon, he was awake again.

"What . . . is it here?" he whispered hoarsely. He was
only half-awake, and it seemed to take forever to make
sense out of where they were and what they were doing.

"No. Look." Uita nodded, not wanting to bring an arm
out from under the robe to point. Where the doorflap had
been there was snow piled up ankle-deep. "It has snowed
a long time now. You told me to wake you up, but I
waited so you could sleep. Now for sure the spotted one
will come."

"Yes. Unless it has already found a place, it will come."
Shutok was stiff from sitting up all night. He dreaded the
cold but he needed to move. "I will go look," he said.
Uita grunted a wordless complaint about the cold air he

let under the robe. After he stood she gathered the hide tightly around her.

Shutok stood at the entrance and filled his lungs, enjoying the sharp, cold bite of clean winter air after the heavy smell of old smoke that was baked into the walls and ceiling of the cave. The tightening in his nostrils meant that his breath was freezing. Snow was falling through a white fog, tiny flakes of ice that were silver and blue in an otherwise dull sky. There was nothing else to be seen and he turned back inside.

That afternoon they watched the snow slowly build up. "I wish there was some way to make the killer come," Shutok said. "It is getting colder."

He was thinking of something but he hesitated. Shutok had grown up knowing that there were many forbidden words. It was against the way to say the cat's name because the animal would hear it and come, but was that not just what they needed now?

"Jaguar," he said. "Jaguar, come here." Then his eyes happened to land on one of the charms the shaman had made for the hunters. It was on a shelf beside him and he reached for it. "That's it," he said, studying the charm.

The boy got up again and went to the corner where the remains of the nest were. He picked out some twigs and grass and went back to Uita.

"What now?" she complained. "Can you sit still, or must you play with sticks and make me freeze?"

"I want to make a charm like this one," he said. "A hunting charm for the jaguar." But the twigs broke when he started to bend them. They were too brittle with age.

"Hair," she said.

"What?"

"Make the charm with hair. Here, I will show you how," and she started to separate a lock of her hair.

"No. I want to do it. It would not be fitting for a girl to make a hunting charm."

"Is it better for a boy?" Uita protested. "Shutok is no shaman."

"Do not start an argument now." He held a lock of his hair in both hands, but he knew it would be impossible for him to pull it out — not just because it would hurt, but because he did not have the strength to pull out so much at once.

"You can pull better than I can," he said. "You do it." Uita took hold of his hair with a sly smile on her face. After she pulled it, hard enough to hurt but not hard enough to pull it out, she laughed out loud at him.

"Ouch! Why didn't you pull harder? Now you will just have to do it again."

"You said to pull it, but I think it would be better to cut it with a scraper." She went to get the sharp stone scraper that they used for skinning, and when she came back with it she said, "Some shaman!"

She cut his hair and that hurt as much as pulling it. Then he wet the hair in the snow. He made it stiff and workable with ashes from the firepit. When he was finished he had shaped it into a charm with four legs. It took imagination, but Shutok was able to see the jaguar quite clearly in the black bundle of knotted hair. After he had admired it long enough he put it on the shelf with the shaman's straw bison.

He was almost sorry to be finished with the charm. They had nothing to do now but wait, and the longer they waited the more Shutok worried that the jaguar might not come no matter what they did. It began to grow darker and Uita complained that they were freezing for nothing.

"The spotted one did not come," she said. "Will you build a fire now?"

"No, let us wait for him one more night. There is much snow. Soon the jaguar must get cold. We should sleep now, so we will be rested if it comes in the night."

Shutok felt warmer as he got sleepier. He looked through half-closed eyelids at the snow. It looked knee-deep now, but he was too comfortable to go find out. The snowflakes were larger, and without the crackling of the fire the afternoon was so quiet that he thought he could hear the snowflakes as they landed outside. There was only the sound of Uita's breath, whistling as she slept, and every now and then the sound of snow pressing into snow.

The boy let his eyes shut for just one heartbeat, then another. That lulling sound of snow falling seemed even closer with his eyes closed. It was better than a murmuring summer stream for putting one to sleep.

Only when Shutok shifted so he could rest his head against the wall beside him, opening his eyes dreamily in the half-light, did he know what he had been hearing. There, already half inside the entrance, was the spotted one. The boy gasped suddenly, as if his breath were being sucked out of him. Then he held it, for the animal froze, one paw suspended in the air like a hawk about to dive. Except for Uita's whistling breath there was silence. The air, when Shutok breathed again, was tainted with a new smell — the sour, carrion odor of the huge cat.

Shutok watched the animal put down its paw. Yet even though he looked closely, the motion seemed disguised by time, like the growing of a plant or the movement of the sun.

Before he thought to wake Uita the animal was inside and lying near the cold firepit, its legs tucked under it in a way that might have been a crouch. Without looking away — without blinking — Shutok touched the girl beneath the robe. The cat's eyes were wide in the dim light, and the boy had the feeling that they could see through the robe. The eyes did not move when Uita stirred, and there was no other sign of readiness in the animal's body. Its mouth and nose were rimmed with frost from its breath. Clumps of ice had hardened on its paws and others hung beneath its heavy breast.

The jaguar was a terrifying sight, and the smell of death that accompanied it was awful, but when Shutok looked into its big expressionless eyes he almost believed that the animal was cold and tired, like someone come to visit with a problem that could be worked out in a friendly way. Then Uita saw the animal and stifled a scream. It escaped from her like the chirp of a bird, and she immediately buried her head in the blanket again. Shutok heard her begin to sing, her voice squeaky and faltering.

"Stop it," he whispered. "And help me." He held his spear with both hands, its shaft running beneath one arm. The end of it was wedged solidly in the crack behind him. "Hold this," he said.

She seemed not to understand. Although she had stopped singing, Uita's head was still hidden, a round bulge in the robe next to the boy's elbow. He did not want to have to coax her now. Shutok hit her sharply in the side of the head with his elbow.

"Do as I say." He did not bother to whisper now. His heart and mind were racing.

The jaguar did not seem to care that they were there. It walked to the far wall and flopped down, then began to lick itself, cleaning the ice from the bottom of one front paw. Stretched out, it was longer than a man was tall, and Shutok thought he could hit it with one of his spears.

"I want you to hold this," he said again. He tried to steady his voice, but his hand trembled uncontrollably as he gave the girl his spear. "Like this, under your arm, and no matter what happens do not let go."

Shutok picked up another spear — the second pole from the door — aimed, and threw it. It was too heavy. He missed. The cat gave him a look that made the boy shrink, and then went on with its bath. Shutok heard the rasping of the animal's rough tongue.

"This will never do," he muttered. "There is not enough room to throw." He picked out another spear and got to his knees. His knuckles scraped on the low ceiling when he cocked his arm.

". Don't," Uita pleaded, but Shutok threw the spear,

wrenching his back. He fell sideways onto Uita with a groan.

The spear hit the floor first, flatly, and slid across the dirt to hit the jaguar in the belly. Shutok had thrown as hard as he could, but the spear did not pierce the animal's skin. With terrible swiftness the jaguar was on its feet, but it did not run away as Shutok had expected. Uita tried to stand, too, and Shutok had to hold her. "Sit down!" he ordered. "There is nowhere to run."

"Stupid!" she answered. "Leave the spotted one alone. Stupid!"

"Shut up and give me your spear." The cat was pacing back and forth in front of them, trying to understand the rows of sharpened stakes that separated it from them. As if talking to itself, it made deep rumbling sounds in its throat, lifting its lips to reveal huge, yellowed teeth. Uita sat down and pulled the robe over her head. She tried to sing but choked on the words.

Shutok saw that the cat would soon discover a way through the stakes. He began to blubber in terror. "Go away," he whimpered. "Just go away. I am sorry I said your name. Please just go away and leave us alone."

He panicked. Still holding onto his spear with one hand, the boy began throwing anything he could reach with the other — dirt, spears, and finally his crutch.

Then there was a horrible, tearing sound that seemed to come from the very rock itself. It was the jaguar, growling, but it sounded as if the rock were closing in on them. Shutok shut his eyes, and he did not open them though he felt himself being thrown, bruised, and cut.

97

Uita stopped screaming long enough to take a breath and then she screamed again. The struggle around him could only mean the worst. Shutok could not look. All the while there was a violent pushing and pulling on the spear, and the smell and feel of blood. Suddenly Shutok's head struck rock. It was only after Uita's screaming stopped completely that he heard the sounds coming from himself. He stopped his moaning and lay still, pretending to be dead.

Shutok shivered in the freezing air. He wondered if he had been sleeping. His ears were still ringing from Uita's screaming. When he opened his eyes he was thinking that perhaps the spotted one had eaten the girl and gone.

But no! There, close to his face, was one of the giant paws. He closed his eyes again and played dead, but his teeth were chattering. He thought the cat was sure to notice. Then something touched him and he squealed.

"Are you alive?" He sat up and Uita's hand stayed on his leg. "No!" she whispered urgently. "The spotted one is not dead." And as if to prove that she was right, the jaguar took a breath that swelled its chest. It let out the breath with a long, low whistle, and a bright bubble of blood appeared at the corner of its mouth.

The cat lay on its side, its front paws folded gracefully as if it were in the middle of a jump. The powerful hind legs were twisted in an unnatural way, though, and this was because the leg beneath the animal was lifted from the ground by one of the sharpened stakes. It had gone deep into the muscle before breaking off.

But that was not the jaguar's only wound. A brown stain spread out in the sand from the animal's neck. The bloody spear beside him told Shutok what had made the cut there. Bright new blood glistened red where the coat was torn and around that the jaguar's yellow and brown fur was dirty-looking where the blood had dried.

Shutok scooted closer to Uita and pulled the bison robe over himself. "What happened?" he asked. The words were hard to form in his mouth. He was so cold that he did not feel any warmth at all beneath the blanket.

"I do not know," she answered. "I closed my eyes and pulled the robe over my head. It sounded like the spotted one was eating you, so I did not look. Then when everything was quiet again I had to look. I thought you were dead. Are you hurt?"

"It is nothing," he answered slowly. He was too cold, he knew; his speech was slurred because the words were stiff in his cheeks. "Just my back, and some bruises. And my head," he added.

Shutok felt his head tenderly, since that was what hurt the most. Beneath the sticky hair he discovered a big bump and broken skin. "Maybe I was knocked out," he said. But he told himself that that was not true. He remembered being too afraid to open his eyes, but he did not say anything about that.

"We should build a fire," he said, meaning that Uita should do it.

"I will not move until the spotted one dies. Look, it runs."

But it only seemed to be running. Still on its side in the

bloody sand, the animal was moving its legs. Shutok's fear of the great killer turned to pity as he watched it. Its eyes looked brittle, as if they must feel like fish scales or dried leaves. The boy felt sure that it was not seeing anything now, but it seemed to be trying to run away from its pain. Shutok was overwhelmed with a dirty feeling, as if he had done something terribly nasty, and he looked away before being sick. Soon it would be too dark to see.

"It would have killed us," he said absently to Uita. "It jumped onto the spear." He heard the animal moving and wanted to help it. For some reason he put his hand to his throat. He could not remember why he had thought to do that.

"Shutok is a great hunter," Uita answered. "To kill this killer of men you must have big power. I am sorry I said many things." There was respect in her voice.

"But I only wanted to make it go away." Shutok began to cry silently. He was exhausted and cold and the killing upset him. "It must be hard to kill all the time. Is that why the hunters never talk about it?" Uita looked at him strangely but she said nothing.

He slept some, but he woke several times during the night and listened to the struggle being lost so close to him. "Die," he begged. "I am sorry, but please die."

Sometime before the first daylight reached through the entrance of the cave to touch it, the great hunter of men stopped moving its legs.

10

UITA POKED the beast with one of the sharpened stakes
to be sure it was dead. Shutok solemnly built a fire. He
went about his task wordlessly. He noticed that Uita poked
the carcass again. When she lifted one of the cat's paws
and playfully let it drop he was angry, angrier with her
than he had ever been before.

"Stop that!" Uita's eyes fell before the glowering look
he gave her and she did not argue. She joined him beside
the fire.

The fire felt so good that Shutok stood too close, singe-
ing his clothes. He built it large, an extravagance since the
wood from the nest was dwindling to nothing. He would
burn the spears, he thought. They had been cold for days
and they deserved a large fire as a reward for their suffer-
ing.

They had been hungry too. Shutok went at last and
laid a hand on the jaguar. He was cautious and his heart
pounded, making him feel giddy with his hunger. The
cat's flesh was hardened in death, but running his hand
over the animal's coarse winter hair was like passing his
hand through flames.

Uita watched him sheepishly. He drew back from the animal and said to her, "Unworthy as we are, we will feast upon the flesh of the spotted one. But it must not be with bragging or laughter. We will honor it as a great enemy, and its flesh will fill us with strength and wisdom and courage."

They ate and grew drowsy, but Shutok would not let himself rest until all the work was done. It was unpleasant for him — not because he was squeamish, but because this was the killer of men and he was merely a boy. Shutok was happy to be alive, but he felt in his heart that something was wrong. Killing the jaguar had been almost accidental, and he had been a coward.

Together they skinned the carcass and staked out the hide so it could be scraped and cured. They went to pains to keep the hide whole, ears and all.

They replaced the doorflap. After they cut the meat they put it just inside the entrance, where it was cold enough to freeze, but where the skin door covered it. Still, it would take watching to keep coyotes or ravens from raiding their winter cache of food, even inside the door. Then they rested beside their fire, made from the last of the nest.

In the morning, after they had put the stakes in the fire and the spears and everything else that would burn except the two door poles, Shutok said, "I am going for wood."

"Wait. I will go too."

They stepped around the meat piled in the entranceway, but then they stopped to look around them in disbelief. The landscape had changed again. Before today the light dustings of autumn snow had given the marsh a clean look. On warm fall days when most of the snow melted, the dull brown view was still brightened by cheerful patches of white that stayed on in the shade. But today snow covered everything except the green undersides of a few trees in the valley. The light assaulted their eyes.

"How will we find firewood?" Uita asked, squinting at Shutok. "It is all under snow. And it is cold. Brr! I think we should go back in the cave now."

"And sit there until it is as cold inside as it is out here? Do you remember how cold you were yesterday?"

Shutok led off through the snow and Uita followed, so closely that the first time he fell she fell with him. The boy scooped up a handful of snow and threw it in her face.

"Watch who you are walking on!" he said, laughing. The scuffle ended only when Uita complained about her wet, red hands.

"My fingers never hurt so bad," she said through clenched teeth. They had to go back to the cave to warm up, holding their hands over the coals of their very last wood.

"When we are warm again we must go back out," Shutok said. "And we cannot play. I will follow you, and if you make good steps in the snow I will not fall."

"I have not seen so much snow before. How long will it stay?"

"I don't know. It cannot last for long," Shutok answered hopefully. "Come on, let's go."

The branches of the trees along the creek were the only

pieces of wood that were not covered up. They gathered these by snapping them off, sometimes swinging Shutok's crutch to reach the higher ones. The branches were small. They worked the rest of the day before collecting enough to last through the night.

"I hope it is easier to find wood tomorrow," Shutok said, watching their dinner cook over a small fire. Uita was singing her song quietly. Shutok listened carefully.

"Is that the only song you know?" he asked.

"You do not like Uita's song?"

"No, no, that is not what I meant. It is the only song that you sing. That is why I asked. What do the words mean?"

"It says, 'I was born near water, at the time of the mosquito,' and then I make the sound of the mosquito."

"Is that all?"

"That is all."

"I don't understand. Why is it your song? Did you make it up?"

"No. My people give songs. A song that is mine belongs to no one else, so no one else can sing it. My mother gave me this song. It means more than words."

"But why should your mother give you a song about mosquitoes? They're just pests." Maybe the only good thing about winter was that there were no mosquitoes, he thought. The rest of the time they drove him to fits.

"Mosquitoes come at end of the long hungry time. We say spring like this: *uitaxamt*. It means 'mosquito hatch.' I was born then, so my mother gave me a happy name, 'springtime.' The first mosquito buzzing is a happy sound, for soon after that we eat roots. The bison come to the river. Then the berries ripen. There is much to eat. *Uitaxulpt* is 'death of the mosquito,' when the hungry time begins. This is *uitaxulpt*, winter. I sing because I do not like winter. I wish it could be springtime now."

"Would you teach me to sing the song? I don't like winter either."

"No. It is bad to do that, like stealing. Sometimes rich men buy songs from one another, because to have many songs is very good. They must pay many robes, or a slave. But maybe I can give you your own song. It will belong to you and after I teach it to you, only you will sing it."

Uita closed her eyes and began to hum something. It was not at all like her song, and not as good, Shutok thought.

"What is it about?" he asked impatiently. Uita stopped humming, opened her eyes, and smiled at him.

"I will tell you when I know," she said lightly. "You must wait."

They ate their dinner then. The meat had a sour taste that was not pleasant. "Shaman," Uita said, wrinkling up her nose. "He spoiled the meat." Shutok gave her a warning look. To hear her speak about the spotted one like that felt the same as breaking the way. He was sure it was not good to make jokes about what had happened.

She was quiet then, and later that night whenever they talked it was not about the song she had promised. Shutok asked her about it in the morning, but she only smiled in a way that told him she was enjoying his curiosity. He decided to stop asking about it.

Wood gathering was difficult, but since they had food

it was their only job. Days passed and the snow grew deeper, but that meant they could reach higher in the trees for branches. As long as they worked together they were able to find enough wood to cook over and to keep themselves from freezing. They never had any wood left over by morning, though, so no matter what the weather was like they had to go out every day.

Then one night the girl said, "I cannot eat any more of this." She threw her dinner into the fire only half-eaten.

"What is wrong with it?" Shutok asked, knowing what the answer would be. She had been complaining about the jaguar meat since the first day she tasted it, but she had never refused to eat it before.

"It tastes rotten."

"But it isn't. We have been eating it every day for how long now? More days than anyone can count. And it has not made us sick." He did not like the taste of it either. Still, it was not right to waste it, and besides that, what else was there to eat? He had said all of this to her before, but it never made any difference. Uita liked to complain.

"Look," she said. She opened her mouth wide and showed him that her teeth were loose by wiggling one of them with her fingers. "Soon my teeth will fall out, and I will look like an old woman."

"That's not because the meat is rotten," he explained. "It happens to my people every winter." He wiggled one of his own front teeth to show her that she was not the only one with bad gums.

"I do not care. I will not eat any more of that," she

said, pointing with disgust to the meat scorching in the fire.

So in the days that followed Uita hunted for rabbits and Shutok gathered wood by himself. The little valley felt foreign to him, as if not just the season had changed, but the place. The boy was lonely. The heavy silence of winter filled him with vague fears and worries. Where was Uita? Could he get back to the cave? The limbs broke off with snaps that seemed to draw attention to where he was. Was he alone? The boy was always looking nervously over his shoulder.

They had fires only at night now. Shutok could not bring enough wood to heat the cave during the day too, when neither of them was there anyway. Each morning he banked the coals beneath a layer of ashes so that they would hold their heat. Then, almost without speaking to each other, the two would go off separately.

Each time he returned with an armload of wood he hoped that Uita would be back early. "Uita?" he asked, brushing past the door. Sometimes she was there with a rabbit, and then she would help him the rest of the day. If there was no answer the boy would stand blinking in the sudden darkness, still hoping that when his eyes adjusted she would be there. If she was not there he threw down the wood and went back for more without pausing to rest.

They gave up looking for the snow to melt. It had blanketed everything since the night of the jaguar. Still, Shutok would never have thought that snow could be so different from one day to the next. It fell loose and powdery. On these days he could not stay dry. Snow froze on his eyelashes and hair. It stuck to his fur clothes and then melted. It found its way up under his clothes when he fell in it. More than anything else about winter, Shutok hated having to fetch wood in new or falling snow.

But there were other kinds of snow. After a hard wind the surface might crust over, and Shutok's feet plunged through at every step — or at every other step, as if one of his legs were shorter than the other. This hurt his back. The sharp crystals of ice cut through his thin skin shoes so that he had to make new ones. But the crust was easier going than deep, soft snow.

There were days of sun too, when the snow was hard and slippery. He became so used to sliding and balancing with his crutch for support that the solid floor of the cave felt strange underfoot. He might sweat on these days, and his face would burn from too much reflected sun. But there were no days that Shutok was sorry to see end. Compared to the daytime, evenings around their tiny fire were warm and cheerful.

"Have you come up with my song yet?" Shutok mumbled one night after a rabbit dinner. It was a hard question for him to ask. She might have changed her mind, he thought.

"No. And I did not forget," she answered. Her voice sounded tired. "But I want it to be right for Shutok. It has not come into my heart yet. You must wait."

At first the boy was hurt. He knew he should not have asked. Why was it so hard for her to give him something as simple as a song? Then another thought came to him. If he gave her a gift, perhaps that would make it easier for her. But what could he give her?

He thought it should be a song. In the morning when he was alone he let his voice out into the dead white silence but he stopped almost as soon as he started. The snow swallowed up his words and left him feeling empty and exposed. "No wonder," he said to himself under his breath. If Uita felt as hollow as he felt now, no wonder his song would not come into her heart.

That afternoon he had another idea. The jaguar pelt lay folded in the corner of the cave where the animal had died. He was frightened of it. Every time he touched the skin he felt the power of the killer run through his fingertips like sparks. He would not let Uita touch it because she had no respect for the spirit of the killer. Everything she said about it made Shutok angry with her.

"We are rich," she said. "More rich than the shaman. Some man will trade everything for such things, wait and see." But to Shutok such talk was unseemly. She understood nothing about the boy's sense of wrongdoing.

The teeth and claws of the animal were on the shelf with the hunting charm he had made out of his hair. Once he would not have considered such a thing, but now he decided that he would use some of them to make a necklace for Uita. It was a good thing to do, he told himself; the power of the killer would protect her when she hunted. He thought with excitement about the night when it would be finished and he could give it to her.

Because he wanted it to be a surprise he worked on it

only when she was not there. He made the necklace by cleaning the marrow from tiny, straight pieces of bone. When he strung these on sinew they became beads. Then, using a bone splinter as a drill, he made holes through four of the jaguar's claws. He spaced these evenly between the bone beads and then marveled at the beauty of his own work.

"Never has anyone of my band owned such a treasure," he told himself. He decided that after he had given this necklace to Uita he would make more, using the teeth too, if he could find a way to drill holes in them.

It had taken him three days to make the necklace between trips for firewood. On the afternoon of the third day he stopped working early to wait for Uita to come. It had been another sunny, almost warm day. She might even have a rabbit, he thought. It made him laugh out loud to admit to himself just how sick he was of jaguar meat.

Shutok was happy. In spite of winter's hardships, everything was good now. If it lasted forever he thought he could be content.

When he saw her coming he could hardly keep from jumping to his feet and walking down to meet her. But he did not want to let on that anything was out of the ordinary. It would spoil the surprise.

She stopped at the creek to break the ice out of the waterhole. When she started up the hill he went to build up the fire. He waited. It seemed to take her forever to climb up the hill.

When Uita stepped inside she looked around blindly

for him. Shutok had not just imagined that it had taken her a long time to come from the creek. She had dropped her spear somewhere along the way. Her arms hung limply at her sides. Beads of sweat stood out around her nose and her face was blistered with sunburn.

"Uita?"

She smiled a weak greeting. Her lips were so dry that the lower one had split and bled. The smile went suddenly out of her face. Then, sitting down just where she had stood, she said, "Uita does not feel good."

11

SHE REFUSED to eat. "The meat makes me sick," she said, looking away squeamishly when Shutok offered her some. The boy had not forgotten about his surprise. He gave it to her, hoping it would cheer up his friend.

"Look, I made something for you. I made it while you were hunting so that it would be a surprise. Do you like it?"

"I like it," she said, taking it from him. Shutok was disappointed. She did not look at it with any interest and she did not put it on. Very soon after that she lay down next to the fire, looking dully into the flames.

"I was hot all day. Now I am cold."

Shutok put more wood on the fire. "What did you do today?" he asked.

"I saw a deer, and because it could not run fast in the snow I chased it. The sun was hot. I took off my heavy robe and ran some more. Then the deer got away and I could not find my clothes before I got cold again. Now I cannot get warm."

"It may be that some evil spirit of the snow saw you,"

Shutok worried. "Let's hope that it is not a strong one. You must try to drive it out."

"How can I do that?"

"I don't know," Shutok admitted. "Rest tomorrow. That will help. And you should eat some of this, even if you don't like it."

Uita groaned and rolled her head away. She began to cough before morning, and when Shutok touched her forehead it was hot like a hearthstone.

The way she coughed told Shutok that he had been right. Some evil spirit of the winter had gone into her chest. She coughed hard, trying to throw the bad one out, but when she stopped coughing to breathe, Shutok could hear it again. It made a sound like the night call of a bird.

He tried to keep her as warm as possible, thinking that the evil might not like the heat. He despaired when the wood ran out before morning. The spirit's voice had gotten louder, even though Uita coughed harder and harder. The boy took off his winter robe and put it over her. Then he went out into the cold black night to see what wood he could find.

That day he raced after wood endlessly. Each time he returned he found that Uita had not moved. Sometimes she was sleeping and he left again. If she was awake she was coughing. Shutok tried to encourage her.

"Just stay there and rest. I think you are better already," he lied. Before leaving he always put part of the wood he had brought onto the fire. He put the rest of it aside to use during the night. The cave was not very warm —

he could see Uita's breath in the cold air — but Shutok knew he had to think ahead now. He could not let the fire go out again.

Throughout the day the sun continued to shine brightly, but without his own warm clothing Shutok knew he was taking a dangerous chance. Uita needed his winter robe more than he did, he thought. But this was how the evil had found its way into the girl. He warily avoided the shadows, thinking that such a bad one would be waiting where it was coldest.

Uita was asleep when he came in with his last load of wood. She was not awake by the time he had cooked something to eat, so he set some of the meat aside where it would stay warm. His heart was dark as he watched her face, crusted around her mouth and nose. She was breathing so shallowly that Shutok could not see her blankets move. Then the demon in her chest choked her and she woke up coughing.

"Uita?" She looked at him, then away, the coughing bending her double. Listening to her cough, Shutok thought of getting just his fingertips under a huge stone and then lifting, getting it almost up and over, and then losing his hold only to let it fall right back into place. That was what she sounded like, trying to get the bad one out. She stopped to gasp for air before starting in again.

When she could breathe more easily Shutok insisted that she eat. Lifting her head, he put a sliver of meat onto her lips, but she would not take it into her mouth. She fought back when he tried to force her lips open, shaking her head from side to side until finally he had to give up. "I want to help you," he said forlornly.

Uita looked at him then, and Shutok was terrified by what he thought he saw in her eyes. They were like deep, forbidding shadows, but way at the back of them was something shimmering like ice. It was the evil, looking out at him. He backed away and it seemed to watch him.

"Uita will die. There is nothing that Shutok can do." The voice that snarled at him was his friend's, but the boy was certain that the evil had made her speak. It had control of her now and it had seen him too. He was relieved when she began to cough again because she closed her eyes.

Without his robe Shutok was too cold to sleep. He kept the fire burning, but in order to make it last all night he had to keep it small. He thought about taking the door apart again so he could sleep under it, but that would only let more cold air in on Uita. Then he remembered the jaguar pelt.

He crawled across the cave to get it but he hesitated before pulling it over his shoulders. The back of his neck was prickly as if something was watching. Turning to look behind him, he saw that Uita was sitting up, that strange light in her eyes.

"I am cold. I am going to cover myself with this," he explained. Uita did not answer. When he put on the spotted robe she looked horrified and crawling out from under her blankets, she moved toward the door.

"Wait! What is the matter with you?" As the boy

hurried on his hands and knees to stop her the pelt slipped off his back. She was weak. Otherwise he would never have been able to hold her. "Don't you know who I am?" he asked when he saw how wildly her eyes fought him. She calmed down and he was able to help her back to the fire.

"Don't be afraid," he said. "I won't put it on again if it scares you." Uita stared through him stupidly as if looking at nothing.

Then in an instant he knew what it was. Uita was not afraid of the jaguar pelt. He remembered that before she got sick he had to keep her away from it. But the evil one inside of Uita *was* afraid of it. He remembered too how the shaman had worn hideous paint and sung dreadful songs in order to drive out evil. Perhaps he could do the same thing.

Shutok waited until she was asleep again. Watching her closely to be sure that the bad one was not looking out at him through her eyes, he drew spots on his face, chest, and arms with soot from the fire. He put the jaguar pelt over himself and pulled the scalp piece low on his forehead. When he was ready he wished he could see what he looked like. The boy could not help thinking that he looked more powerful than the shaman had looked in his paint and his robe of bird skins.

He waited until Uita woke up coughing. When she saw him he had to sit on her to hold her down.

"I know you're there," he said to the spirit in her eyes. He began to sing. Shutok did not know any medicine songs so he sang war songs and hunting songs. They were loud, but the boy worried that they were not ugly enough to make Uita's evil want to leave her. He began making up songs of his own, forcing his voice to make great, shrill leaps from one nonsense word to another. She struggled and tried to look away, but Shutok held his face close to hers and made horrible faces. He felt cruel, but when Uita coughed so hard that sweat broke out on her forehead, the boy thought he was winning. The more the spirit protested, the more vicious he became until Uita suddenly closed her eyes and lay very still.

"Oh no!" he exclaimed. For a moment the boy thought he had scared her to death. He put his ear to her mouth and listened. When he heard her breathing he began to cry with relief. He went to sleep wondering if he had done more harm than good.

In the morning Uita's fever was high. Her skin seemed to glow with heat. Sometimes after she had cleared her lungs enough to breathe more easily she prattled deliriously in her own language. Once when Shutok asked her what she was saying she answered him.

"Too hot. Uita want to go out in snow," she said. She tried to throw off her blankets but she was too weak.

"No. You stay covered up," he said gently. He reached down to brush a few stray hairs off her sticky forehead. "The spirit wants you to go outside because it does not like the heat. Soon it will go away and you will get better." But he did not believe himself. He looked away to blink back his tears. The necklace was in the dirt by the firepit. Shutok wanted her to have it, so he lifted her head and arranged it around her neck.

"I have to go out for wood," he said. He was certain she did not understand him, but he wanted to talk to her anyway. "Would you like a drink of cold water before I go?" he asked, reaching for the waterskin.

"Yes."

"You answered me! Now I know you're better. Is there anything else I can get you? Are you hungry?" But she began to cough. Although she took a drink Shutok could not get her to speak to him again. Still, he was encouraged, and when he went for wood he went with strengthened steps.

Again and again Shutok went to the trees by the stream, broke off what branches he could reach, and carried them up the hill to the cave. He got there winded and panting, but after he stepped inside he held his own breath until he could hear Uita's. It was there like the sound of a breeze blowing through dry summer grasses. The boy's heart felt as if it would pound a hole in his chest when he finally breathed again.

She slept all day. Even when Shutok felt her forehead she did not wake up. It was not as hot to the touch and her color was more natural, though pale. "I did it." Shutok wanted to shout, but he whispered. "I did it. I drove the evil one away."

Then, sometime in the middle of the night, it happened. Shutok was asleep, but he woke up and heard her sneeze twice. He looked over at her and saw that she was on her side looking back at him.

"I am hungry," she said. "Will you cook?"

Uita's fever left her, but she had a runny nose and cough that lasted day after day. She was so weak that Shutok fed her. Then, as she got stronger, she was cranky because he babied her too much.

"I will help you bring wood," she said when the weather turned bad again. Shutok was having a hard time gathering enough fuel, but he made her stay inside. She was still complaining about the taste of the meat, and he was afraid that she would start to argue about hunting if he let her go out.

"No, I can get it myself. You just stay beside the fire and rest."

"Nothing to do here. I want to go outside."

"It is too cold. Look, it is snowing again. Maybe when it stops."

"It will never stop," she said glumly. "It will snow forever."

"No, it won't," Shutok replied without conviction. The return of nasty weather made them both gloomy. "I am going out now. You stay here."

But Uita was as headstrong as ever. That afternoon Shutok was dragging a heavy limb up the valley when he saw her at the waterhole. She was bent over the water looking at her reflection, her heavy bison robe pulled down so that her shoulders were bare. He dropped the branch and stormed over to her.

"I came for water," she said.

"Then where is the waterskin?" he demanded. She looked caught and pulled the robe tight around her neck. "Don't you know better than to let the cold touch your skin? That is the way the evil found you before."

"I wanted to look at something," she admitted. The look in her eyes was mysterious, then impatient as she waited for him to understand. Shutok stood wondering what she was talking about. Then it came to him and he was embarrassed. She had been admiring her necklace.

"Why don't you help me with this branch?" he stammered, but he was pleased, more pleased than if she had said thank you.

For the next several days she was as mysterious. The boy was made uncomfortable by the way she seemed to be expecting him every time he came in with wood. She answered him so shortly when he stopped to warm up that he wondered why she did not want to talk. Then she might say, "I am cold. We do not have enough wood for the night yet. Go quickly." The boy understood that she wanted him to leave her alone, but he did not know why until he sneaked back once and heard her. Then, not wanting to spoil her surprise, Shutok hurried away again.

He listened carefully after that. Occasionally during the next couple of days he heard her as he approached the cave, but the singing either stopped or she changed her song as soon as she knew he was coming.

Then one night after they had eaten she began singing the song that was oddly familiar to him by now. Although she was singing and smiling at the same time, Shutok tried not to show anything but curiosity in his face. There were a few words in his language, but most of the song he could not understand, making it seem secret and deep. More than that, the song was special because of the places it went in her voice. The boy thought immediately of the nonsense songs he had made up to drive away the snow demon when Uita had been so sick.

"What song is that?" he asked when she was finished. He held his face rigid, trying to show the dignity that was fitting when receiving a gift, but his voice revealed his excitement.

"It is Shutok's song," she replied. For a drawn-out moment they looked at each other without speaking. It was not awkward; there just seemed to be nothing to say. Uita's smile was bright, although in better light the boy knew that her gums would look black like his own. Her face was thinner, cheekbones and jaw sharp, drawing attention away from her crooked eyes.

"Shutok will learn it now," she said. She sang it again and then told him to try, but Shutok hesitated after an awkward start.

"What does it mean?" he asked. "It would be easier for me to learn if I knew what the words meant first." She bit her lips in the pause that followed, distant and thinking. Then she explained.

"Before, when I tried to make a song, nothing came. I

thought about Shutok and the killer, and then inside it felt like it was all happening again. But no words came and no song. Just feelings. Sorry."

"That's all right. I think I understand." He told her about singing outside, and about the way the snow seemed to swallow up his voice.

"Then when I was sick something happened. A dream maybe, but maybe not. The killer came. It looked real and then sometimes it looked like Shutok. I was very afraid, so that my heart seemed to stop, my breath to fly away. So some of the song says that."

"Why did you make it in your language and not mine?"

"Because I do not talk so good in your language. It was easier. And to ask you to help would spoil the surprise."

"Tell me what the rest of it means."

"I know that you have big power from the killer. It feels like the spotted one is always around you. The song says that. The rest of it sounds the way the spotted one talks, the best I know. Now it is like magic, like a shaman song, and I feel a bigness inside when I sing it. You try."

She repeated the song until he learned it. Very late into the night the girl said, "You know the song. I will not sing it again. It belongs to you now." She lay down on her side of the fire and Shutok had to stop singing so she could sleep.

But the song was loud in his head. He was too happy to sleep just yet.

12

SHUTOK'S SONG was his companion whenever he left the cave. His voice no longer sounded lonely and small. Instead, winter and its silent evils seemed to stand a bit farther back from him, as if the song really were magic. It lifted the boy's spirits on bad days, when he fell, or when the wind swirled new snow in his face and up under his clothes. On good days he rejoiced with it, feeling recklessly strong and carefree.

And the song began to change. At first he tried to sing it exactly the way Uita taught him, but as the days passed the boy found himself making it more his own. The words still told about the jaguar, but alone, outside, the song seemed to turn him inside out, so that his deepest feelings came from his mouth, not merely words and melody. He sang his loneliness for his family. He sang his hatred for the shaman, whom he blamed for causing them to leave him here. He sang the injustice of the pain that crippled him. And Uita, their happiness, their eagerness for spring, all that was in the song too. By the time Uita was well enough to go outside again the song had become so personal that he could not sing it if she accompanied him on his chores. He sang only when he was alone, only when he could give full vent to all his emotions.

Winter became a dispiriting routine that affected Uita more than Shutok. "When spring comes, I will leave here and not come back," she liked to say.

"Didn't it snow along the river?" Shutok asked. He did not want her to talk about leaving. It hurt him to think that she did not want to stay with him after all they had gone through together.

"Yes, but there the snow goes away again. It lasts forever here."

Except for the time he had asked about her mosquito song, Uita had not talked much about her home or her people, although Shutok knew from the way she sang sometimes that she was thinking of them. Now he ventured, "Do you really want to go home all that badly?" He was hoping she would say, "Not really."

"As soon as the snow melts I will go."

"But why?" he exploded. Then he remembered his own loneliness for Ala and Yaiya. "It is because you miss your family, isn't it? But are my people so different from yours that you could never come to like them?"

"I like Ala already, and you. But I do not want to be a slave, so I will run away before Aar and the others come here again."

"But you are not a slave now. You belonged to the shaman. If he is dead, you don't belong to anyone."

"Not now. But when Aar comes back he will make me a slave again." And the boy knew she was right.

*

Their first sign of warmer weather came as a surprise. One afternoon Uita looked across the marsh to see clouds stacked up violently on the horizon. A winter storm always came fast, many times without a puff of wind to warn them that it was on its way. She pointed it out to Shutok and they headed for shelter, expecting another blizzard.

"What is that?" Uita asked a short time later. They were sitting in the dark, saving their wood until they needed it the most.

"Do you mean that sound? The storm has got here, that's all."

"It sounds different." She pulled aside the doorflap to look out just as Shutok recognized what he was hearing. "Come see," she said. "It rains."

"Like a stampede," he observed. Uita cupped her hand to catch some of it. Shutok shuddered. Rain splattered up from the hard-packed snow onto his shins and he stepped back. He felt colder instead of warmer.

During the night the rain turned briefly to snow again, but the thaw had definitely started. After that everything was wet. The floor of the cave was damp and the dampness crept into Shutok's back, making him stiff and cranky. Water condensed on the walls and dripped. Their firewood put out more smoke than light or heat and their clothing was never dry.

"I would rather have it snow," the boy grumbled.

"No," Uita disagreed. "Soon we will find snow lilies. We can eat the blossoms and bulbs, and throw out that rotten meat."

"Hmm," Shutok grunted. That was a happy thought, not having to eat any more of the sour meat. It was beginning to discolor, and he knew that she was right — it was spoiling.

"I have a feeling that spring is still a long way off, though. It is going to get worse before we can stop eating it." He thought of his family as he spoke. Last year they had had to chew hides in order to survive. Any meat, even rotting meat, was better than hunger grinding like two stones in the belly. He and Uita had been lucky. Shutok knew that his own people might well have starved.

But the boy took heart as each new day brought small signs of change. He remembered how the rough hand of winter had seemed to grip the landscape suddenly and firmly. Overnight the snow had made the little valley above the marsh almost unrecognizable. Spring came differently, taking the land back from winter in a gentle and gradual exchange.

First to appear were the tops of small trees and hardy brush. Bent over beneath the weight of the snow and buried all winter, they sometimes jumped up startlingly into freedom as Shutok and Uita walked past them. Patches of ground emerged, beginning at the base of the cliff and beside boulders and spreading outward, so boggy that they learned to avoid them. The stream ran high and the water was gritty to drink except early in the morning. Crossing anytime was dangerous. The sun grew warmer, the days longer, but the snow lingered tenaciously, dirty and icy in the shade, blindingly bright and mushy in the open.

Then, even before the first flower appeared, they lost what remained of their food. They were coming back to the cave with heavy loads when they saw the bear. It was already into their meat cache.

"It's not a big bear," Uita whispered.

"Big enough," he answered with a warning. They dropped their loads with a clatter. The bear turned its head to look at them, but then went back to its feast. They hid in a muddy patch of dirt that had melted out by a boulder. There was nothing they could do but wait.

It ambled off after a time. "Well, the meat wouldn't have lasted much longer anyway," Shutok said, watching it go. "Springtime can't be far off now if the bears are out."

"I am not sorry the bear ate it. I will hunt again." Now that it was gone, Shutok regretted complaining so often about the taste of the meat.

They ate rabbits and built smaller fires again. There were hungry days, and Shutok missed the girl's company. Still, their surroundings were changing and it was not a dismal season. It became a game to point out every minute detail of spring, both of them testing and stretching their senses in an attempt to outdo the other.

"Did you see the geese today?" she asked, and of course he had.

"I heard the first songbird when I was down by the creek," he told her another day.

"Look," they said, pointing to the greening of the grasses, and later to the insects underfoot.

"I brought you this branch. See, it's budding already."

"Come. I found a lily. I will show you where."

Nothing escaped their notice: the snow creeping back, the clearing of the stream, the appearance of each animal and plant. And by the time Uita showed him the first mosquito bite on her arm, the last lean days of winter were long over. In this season Uita carried her sharpened stick, not for hunting, but for digging. After a winter of nothing but meat, they preferred eating roots and bulbs. The starchy plants soon began to fill out their faces again. Their gums healed. Shutok felt stronger and he assured Uita that his back was better.

"See, I can stand without the stick to hold me up," he said, adding, "When they come back they will see that they were wrong." For every day now the boy's thoughts circled around his family, returning him bitterly in his memory to the night they let the shaman drive him from the cave, then carrying him forward in his imagination as he fancied the way he would greet them.

"I am going to use the crutch less and less each day, so that when they come I will be walking without it again," he confided. "And we must have plenty of food. We will watch for them when the time comes, so that a feast will be ready when they first step into our camp."

"How long before the others come?" Something about the way Uita asked reminded Shutok that she had plans of her own.

"They have started by now," he answered truthfully. As if they might be within sight already, she walked to the hunters' rock and looked out over the marsh. "It will take them more walks than anyone can count before they reach the river," he said. "And you know how far it is from there." She was turned away from him and he left her there to mull things over, searching his own mind for things he might say when she decided to go.

That was not the last time she asked the question, "How long before the others come?" But for the time being she seemed to have concluded that there was no need to leave just yet. The trees leafed out, and when it was warm enough they moved their cooking fire out to the pit in front of the cave. Shutok was encouraged when she made suggestions that were forward-looking.

"We will dry roots now so there will be food when the mosquito dies again," she said. They gathered roots until it seemed they were greedy to dig so many. After the roots dried they wrapped them in skins and buried them in the cave, marking the spots with stones. Shutok began to think that Uita had no intention of leaving, only to hear her ask once more, "How long now?"

"A long time yet," he answered. "But they might be getting close to the river."

"We'll stack wood where the nest was." They made a pile big enough to placate the spirit of the nest-builder, if it was watching, and then added more.

"How long?"

Shutok liked to sit at the hunters' rock now whenever Uita let him rest from the chores she thought up endlessly. Except from here, the greening of the trees cut off the view of the marsh basin. He was sitting by the rock the day he finally admitted to her, "It could be soon."

He knew he should watch her face because it would tell him more than anything she might say, but even as he told her his eyes were pulled away from the girl to the marsh and then vividly beyond. They were out there, somewhere, coming closer, the hunters running lightly and without effort, four of them now with Yaiya, followed by Ala and Mato and Tuta, bent forward beneath their loads. Sitting here at other times, Shutok had almost felt the prairie underfoot, the grass against his legs, the wind, rich with the smells of bison, brush against his cheeks. Today Uita brought him out of his reverie before it took him that far.

"And what will you do with the pelt of the spotted one?"

"What do you mean? I will show it to them." He thought he might even wear it. The hunters, especially Yaiya, would have to respect him after they had seen it. "They will see that I am a hunter, too."

"Hide it."

"What's wrong with you?" Shutok confronted her. He had not minded digging and drying the roots or stacking the firewood, because it had meant that she was staying. But this was different. She was just being bossy, meddling where she had no business. He had waited a long time and he was not going to let her spoil this homecoming for him.

"Hide it now, before the others come and take it from you."

"They wouldn't do that. Those things belong to me."

"You forget maybe? They left you here to die! When they come again, they will take everything away. That is why I hide food for you. They will come back and you will have to sneak scraps of food from camp like a coyote. You will not come here to the rock like this, or come into the cave at night to sleep. You are stupid to forget all this."

"You don't know what you're talking about. It will be different now." He had assumed that they would be happy to see him and he did not want to think anything else.

"Shutok is a fool!"

"Shut up!" he shouted. She stared obstinately back at him as if she had more to say, so Shutok hobbled away indignantly, shouting back over his shoulder that she could leave if she wanted to. He was staying, and there would be a big celebration when they saw that he had survived the winter.

He sulked for days. She ignored him and continued to put food aside, burying it all over the camp like a squirrel. Whenever they exchanged glances, hers was so knowingly smug that the boy went off to sit by the rock from morning until night, watching, showing her that he could be just as stubborn as she.

One afternoon, soon enough after this last quarrel that he was still pouting about it, the boy awoke from a nap with the feeling that something was wrong. He had been sitting with his back up against the warm rock before he drifted off, but when he woke up he was lying down, curled up with his cheek on the ground. It had been a deep sleep, and he had dreamt about the jaguar again. But that was not what woke him.

When his eyes popped open he was so suddenly awake

that he first thought something was watching him. He did not move, sensing danger. When he finally sat up it was just in time to see Uita step from the cave. She was carrying something. Before she had taken more than a few steps Shutok recognized the bundle. It was the hide from the doorway. She saw him looking but did not stop.

"What is that?" he shouted after her, struggling to his feet. "Where are you going?" He fell and it hurt. He gasped in pain. That stopped her, but briefly.

"Look there. They are coming," she said, flushed, the words catching in her throat.

Shutok ignored the wrenching in his back as he gathered legs and crutch beneath him to stand. He looked into the marsh basin quickly, saw nothing on his first glance, then looked back to see that Uita had vanished.

"Uita! Come back here!" he shouted, angry because he was confused and because she was not there to explain.

There was no answer from the girl, but by then he was not listening for one anyway. He saw them. They were much closer than he had expected, already at the edge of the open water on the left-hand side of the marsh. He counted. All the fingers on his right hand and two more on his left. The right number. He could almost see their legs striding toward him.

The shock took away his wind, but when he had filled his lungs again he started to sing. Singing was the language of his heart, and his heart was as big as the sky.

Then he stopped. This was not at all how he had planned it. "I have got to get ready! I shouldn't have gone to sleep. They are so close now there isn't time," he muttered, almost hopping on his crutch in his hurry to get to the cave. "And where did Uita go?"

When he got to the cave he thought he knew. "Thief! So now you run away, and steal everything, too. If I catch you, I'll . . ."

Outside again, confusion and rage spinning him around like a dancer in a frenzy, he did not know which way to go after her. "Uita!" he growled, his throat raw.

"I am here." The boy turned to his right and saw her stepping breathlessly around the cliff. The bundle was gone.

"What did you do with my things? Bring them back."

"I hid them where the crack runs up the cliff. There is a place there, back under a big boulder. It's dry. I wrapped everything so the mice cannot eat it. It's covered with rocks. I will go now. Good-bye, Shutok."

"What? Wait!"

She was crying. "I don't want to be a slave. I will run away now. Good-bye." But she made no move to go, as if her legs would not carry her. "Good-bye," she said again, but instead sat down on the spot and sobbed.

"What? I don't understand any of this," Shutok moaned. He started toward Uita. She was slumped at the top of the trail that led down to the creek, but he didn't get to her before the hunters suddenly walked into camp, silently and from three sides.

THE HUNTERS APPROACHED them with their weapons in their hands and Shutok knew at once why they had surrounded the camp. Seeing smoke from the fire, they could not have known who might be living in the cave. After all, he was supposed to be dead, and, the last they knew, Uita had gone to live with the shaman. The men lowered their weapons as soon as they recognized him, but Shutok felt that the warmth of his greeting was one-sided.

"Hello, Yaiya! Aar, Gan, Hnit, where are the others? Are you hungry? There is food in the cave and . . ." Shutok broke off. First there was disbelief, then suspicion in their faces. They inspected the camp with wary eyes. Uita sat looking at her hands. No one spoke again until Gan strode with powerful steps to the cave, looked inside, and signaled with a shrug that no one else was there.

Yaiya said to the men, "He speaks to us as if he were a hunter. He still has not learned the way." He strutted arrogantly across the camp, waved to Ala, Mato, and Tuta that it was safe, and, leaning on his long spear, struck a dramatic, conquering pose. Shutok thought he observed a look of torment in Aar's eyes. In this respect Yaiya had not changed at all, or at least not for the better. But Shutok noticed with envy that his brother was taller, and his voice deeper. Nevertheless, his brother's foolishness and intrigues were as dear to him as anything in the world.

Ala stopped short when she saw him and the boy heard the catch in her breath. Was she sick? Uita ran to her.

"And Uita too!" his mother exclaimed. The color returned to her face and she asked, narrowing her eyes, "But is this a ghost I see?" When she held out her arms to him Shutok forgot his plans for walking without his stick. He went to her and she hugged him so tightly that his breath was squeezed out of him. He was limp in her arms and he would have collapsed in a pile if she had let him go.

"Evil or not, Shutok would never have made a hunter," he heard Yaiya say. "Look at this mamma's boy." His voice was deeper but it had not lost its sarcastic whine.

"Mato?" Ala asked. "What mother would not be happy to see her young after so long a time, and given up for dead, too?" Mato did not answer, but then Ala was not talking to her. She was talking indirectly to the hunters. Then Shutok, his face still buried in his mother's breast, sensed her go tense. The boy looked up to see Aar standing menacingly over him.

"He should have died. How could such a one live except by evil?" The hunter's face was full of hatred. "And the girl," he went on. "What is she doing here?"

Shutok began to explain. "She went with the shaman but the spotted . . ." He stopped when Ala laid a warning hand

135

on his arm. It was all beginning to seem like a bad dream. Because the way was so strict he could not make the hunter hear him out. He could only listen and obey, no matter how terrible it became.

"The necklace." Gan, Shutok's father, the man whose voice was so seldom heard that the boy hardly knew it, had spoken. Shutok looked around just as Uita put her hand to her throat. She had forgotten to take it off when she hid the rest.

But no, Shutok told himself. That was not it at all. She left the necklace around her neck because she was taking it with her. Right up to the last moment Uita had intended to run away. She had hidden the jaguar pelt just to protect him. She had done everything else just for him, too, until she had finally stayed too long.

"Where did you get it, girl?" Ala asked.

"It is Uita's."

"Did you steal it from the shaman?"

"No. The shaman is dead."

"Then where did you get it?" Ala's voice was gentle, but her eyes were covetous.

"Give it to me," Aar said, stepping up to her. "I have never seen such claws." Uita pulled away but the man grabbed her. He laughed when she fought back, kicking and trying to squirm free. Then he slapped her and Shutok went wild.

"Leave her alone!" he snarled. With the uncontrollable power and speed of a branch pulled back and snapped loose, Shutok hit Aar with his crutch. He wanted to kill the hunter, but his own force threw him to the ground.

Aar grunted but did not let go of Uita. He tore the necklace from her neck, sending bone beads and claws out in a spray. Then he turned on the boy.

"I will teach you respect for the way!" The first kick knocked the wind out of Shutok. Uita was on Aar's back now, biting and scratching, but the hunter kicked Shutok again and again. The boy writhed on the ground gasping hollowly for air like a dying fish, and Aar might have killed him had it not been for Ala and Yaiya.

"And this is our leader, Mato! Will we sing a victory song when he has killed the boy?" Ala began to sing derisively.

Yaiya said soberly, "It is not fitting."

"And what do you know, you howling coyote?" Aar said, facing Yaiya. Uita slid off the man's back and went to Shutok. "You should learn to keep your mouth shut," the hunter threatened. Yaiya blinked but Aar did not strike him. "Tie the girl. And you, Mato, pick up the beads. They are mine now." He stalked off, Gan and Hnit following at a respectful distance.

"You see? You see?" Uita repeated, helping Shutok to sit. Her tears fell big and wet on his shoulder.

Yaiya walked over to them. "Come on. You heard what he said."

"I will help Shutok across the stream to the other camp," Uita said.

"No, I will help him," Ala said. "You go with Yaiya. And let us hope that you will not be tied too tightly —

137

tight enough that you cannot get loose, but not so much that it hurts." She gave Yaiya a glance to see that he understood.

"Come on." Yaiya took Uita by the arm but she shook herself free.

"I do not need anyone to hold me." Yaiya pushed her toward the cave and she went.

"And you should have died when you were supposed to!" Yaiya spat down at Shutok before swaggering off.

"Do not listen to Yaiya. You know the way he is. Aar has had nothing but trouble with him. Not because he is bad, or a coward — he just never thinks. Aar blames me, but it is his age. He will get over it. Now, do you think you can walk?" Ala handed Shutok his crutch and helped him to his feet.

"Yaiya is right. That is why you left me here — to die."

"We left you here because you could not go with us. And do not think that we felt no grief because of it. We are happy to see you."

"That is right, Shutok." Mato was picking up the beads and putting them back on the broken string. Shutok could not tell for sure, but she looked big again. "Many nights I thought with a heavy heart about what happened. Aar does not understand. I do not bear young easily. The death of the child was not your fault."

Shutok inhaled sharply and his face twisted with emotion. He did not want to cry so he said nothing.

"Come on," Ala said. "I will get you settled in the other camp."

They went down the trail together, waded the creek,

and climbed the other side of the valley to the open spot where Shutok had spent so much time the summer before. It was going to be just as it had been, or worse, with him watching his family from a distance, an outcast. At the sight of the ugly, cold firepit, where he had huddled on so many miserable nights, Shutok finally gave in to despair. He cried.

"But it is a miracle that you survived. How is it that you did not starve? We barely had enough ourselves, with all of us looking for food, and it is impossible that you should have eaten." Ala was gathering wood for a fire, chattering while she worked, trying to cheer Shutok up.

Shutok asked what was on his mind. "Does Aar really think I am so evil?"

Ala stopped what she was doing and sat next to him. "Aar is our leader. There are many decisions he has to make, and in all of them he has to guard the way. Everything that happens has a cause, and when he sees what has happened to you he believes it is because you have done something to let the evil in. Aar is only trying to protect us all."

"And do you believe . . ."

"It is not my place to question the way. Nor is it yours. Without the way, how could anything be?"

"Uita's people, the marsh people, they do not have the way."

"They have a way of their own. We do not respect them because it is a way different from ours. But enough of this. Tell me now how it is that you survived, and why Uita is here with you."

The boy began to tell her. He told her Uita's story about the spotted one chasing the shaman and eating him. Shutok was warming to his tale, pride swelling in him as he told her of their preparations for the killer, when he noticed something that stopped him.

"Ala . . ."

"What is it?"

"Look, coming up the trail."

"More than anyone can count!" she whispered.

"And look who is leading them."

"Yes, I see. The shaman."

Ala peeked nervously around the corner of the boulder. She pulled her head back and held her cheek against the stone, her breathing shallow and fast.

"Did they see us?" Shutok whispered.

"Yes, but when they got to the waterhole all of them turned up the trail to the cave." She looked searchingly into Shutok's face. The wrinkles around her eyes were deep with worry.

"Will they fight?" he asked, hoping she would look away. He knew that she was thinking about what he had told her — that the shaman had been eaten by the man-killer. Shutok squirmed before she answered his question.

"Maybe not, if we give them the girl." She moved her head away from the stone and Shutok saw the imprint of it on her cheek. Her eyes left his face. "They must have seen us come around the marsh today. We made no effort to hide. If Aar tells the shaman the story you just told me, that he ran away and lost the girl, he will say that Aar is lying — that it was a trick. And there is no proof. They probably think that the girl went with us, and is only now coming back. No matter what Aar says they will call him a liar. It might be better to fight than to have the hunters lose face like this."

"But there are too many of them."

"Yes, there are too many." Her eyes came accusingly back to his. "I must go. Do not follow me."

"But I can explain!"

"No one would listen. You would only cause them to fight for sure. If you want to help, stay here. Or go hide somewhere."

"Ala . . ."

But she was gone. The boy rolled over onto his bruised ribs to watch her go. He thought he could hear voices above the babble of the stream. Were they fighting already? He had to see.

Stiff from Aar's kicks and scarcely trying to conceal himself, Shutok climbed his side of the valley until he could look across at the scene unfolding in the camp. It was too far to see faces, but there was no mistaking the shaman, gesticulating wildly before the tight cluster of people standing defensively just outside the mouth of the cave. Fanned out in a half-circle were the shaman's men, so many of them that they did not care to take cover.

"They don't have to fight. All they have to do is wait until we run out of water," he said, including himself in the group trapped at the cave.

The shaman taunted the hunters. He ran at them, then back to the safety of his own men. Ala had been right: whatever Aar had told them had not been enough to make them go away. And the shaman had nothing to lose by lying. If he could provoke a fight — one that he was certain to win — there were more slaves to be captured than one girl.

"But I can prove he is lying!" He could show them the jaguar pelt. It would at least prove that there had been a killer of men. And what harm could it do? he thought, reflecting on Ala's warning to stay away.

Going downhill was always harder than going up. Shutok lowered himself on bruised muscles, gritting his teeth with each painful, awkward step. His path took him slantwise down to the bottom of the valley, where he crossed the creek, then uphill on the other side. He did not stop until he stood beneath the rimrock looking for Uita's cache.

He found it so easily that he thought it could not be such a good hiding place. "A big crack in the wall, with a boulder wedged in it," he said, recognizing the spot from Uita's description. The cave was close, just around a shoulder of rock farther down to the right. He listened for voices, heard none, then started up the last part of the climb to the cache.

He had taken only a few steps when, instantly, all his concern for his family in battle, all his resentment for the way Aar had misunderstood and mistreated him, all his worry about Uita, and all his uncertainties about what he was going to do after he walked up to the shaman with the jaguar pelt — all thoughts but one — went suddenly out of his mind. A rattlesnake was coiled in front of Shutok, and his single thought was to hold perfectly still.

The snake did not strike. Sweat ran into the boy's eyes, stinging, clouding his vision. He was afraid to blink. Ala had told him more times than anyone could count that a snake would go away if he stood still long enough. It had been good advice up until now. This snake was different. With its head swaying back and forth it stretched itself higher into the air, its tongue darting nastily.

He was so close to Uita's hiding place that he could see it in the upper edge of his vision without taking his eyes off the snake. The ground showed where she had taken rocks to cover it. He wondered why the snake had not been disturbed by that. And why was it standing up to him so stubbornly?

"They only want to warn you." That was what Shutok had always heard the others say. "A snake is just as afraid of you as you are of it." This snake did not withdraw. Shutok stood still so long that his shadow appeared to lengthen even as he watched it, and the animal's wicked, flat head remained poised to strike. It seemed to insist that he make the first move.

The boy knew better than to try to kill it. It was too close. Forcing his muscles to break the bonds of fear that restrained them, Shutok took a cautious, probing step backward. "Ttttt!" The animal's tail vibrated, producing a raspy, strident buzz that made his skin prickle all over. He could not stop now. Shutok brought his other foot back, then his crutch, and kept moving away from the snake until he was out of danger.

He breathed more easily now, but the snake still barred his way. "Why do you keep me from the things that are mine, brother snake?" he asked. "I have to get past you so that I can try to save my people. Move now or I will kill you."

Shutok stooped for a stone to throw, but before he could pick it up the rattlesnake crawled toward him. The boy was frightened, his bold words meaningless. Never before had a snake acted so aggressively. "What is the matter with you? Go away!" he bellowed, retreating farther downhill.

"What am I supposed to do, then?" Tremors undermined the boy's voice. The snake coiled, lifting its head into a threatening position although Shutok was standing too far away to be within striking distance.

"I will not run away and hide the way Ala told me to do." He lifted his eyes once more to look at the cache. "If only I had the pelt!" he boasted. "I would wear it and show the shaman who has power. Then, snake, you would see how I can stand up to . . ."

Shutok did not finish his sentence. When he brought his eyes back to where the snake had been, it was not there. He looked all around him, but the snake had vanished.

"What is this now?" he said. "Nothing can just disappear like that. It's . . . like *magic!*" But the path was open now, and he had no time to spare thinking about a rattlesnake. He uncovered the cache. The pelt was wrapped inside the bison robe, along with two more necklaces he had made. The shaman was greedy. Perhaps if he gave him the necklaces and the valuable spotted skin the man would be satisfied.

"Ttttt!" Shutok could not hold still this time. He scuttled away from the snake, but bumped his head on the boulder. He was trapped. At his feet the deadly animal was coiled again, its wedge-shaped head cocked like a spear in a hunter's arm. He closed his eyes, waiting for the bite.

The insight came then, like tinder that suddenly bursts into flame after smoking so long. Shutok opened his eyes wide, hoping to see the snake once more, but he was not surprised to see that it had vanished again. The sign! He had been given the sign!

"I understand now," he said. "Are you still watching somewhere?" He looked for the Master, who could take any shape he pleased, and when he saw a bird looking back at him from a tree he spoke to it. "I am supposed to stand up to the shaman, the way the snake stood up to me. I will not be afraid." The bird flew away. Shutok felt he would never again give in to the weakness or the fear within him.

He did not go straight to the cave. A new sense of direction guided him to return without reckless haste to his own camp on the other side of the creek. It was near sundown when he got there. The little clearing was already in shade, and the first chill breeze of evening blew down the valley, ruffling leaves and unsettling the mosquitoes momentarily. He sat by the cold firepit, unused since the day his family abandoned him in the fall, drawing the rosette pattern of the spotted one on top of his goose bumps and mosquito bites with damp charcoal. Finished, he put on the necklaces of teeth and claws, pulled on the jaguar pelt, and then went to the creek to look at himself.

The image that looked back at him from the water was so powerful that Shutok was spellbound. The skullcap was pulled low on his forehead so that none of his own hair showed. The pelt was a mantle of sunlight. The spots on his cheeks, chest, and arms were distinct against his skin, and the necklaces bristled around his neck. But what bewitched Shutok were the beast's eyes — his own eyes reflected back — penetrating, possessed eyes. When he stole up to the camp he was not a boy stalking like a jaguar. Shutok *was* a jaguar, just as a hunter in a power trance became a wolf when he approached the bison herds.

Wanting to enter the camp from above rather than from below, he crept as stealthily as he could through the underbrush, avoiding the trail. He paused to study the camp and to catch his breath at a spot near the hunters' rock. The marsh people were scattered. Two of them sat just in front of Shutok with their backs toward him, and the others sat or stood, not one of them looking particularly warlike.

Still, just the sight of so many men was enough to overawe the boy. He felt the vigor of the trance leave him, radiating away like the heat of a red-hot coal winking out. Neither the shaman nor any of his own people were visible to him, so it was possible that they were in the cave together, having settled their differences. Perhaps the whole silly scheme was not necessary after all, he thought.

He waited. It was chilly, the last rays of the sun only seeming to make it warm. Shutok cursed himself for mistaking a rattlesnake as the sign. He felt more foolish about this than about anything he had ever done. When the sun went down he was ready to leave.

Then one of the dark shapes on the other side of the camp stood up. Shutok was filled with hatred, recognizing the shaman. The man called the others to him with a wave of his arm and the boy realized that they had been waiting for night. Bats were already in the air. Why had his power abandoned him now? he asked himself in despair. This was the time to act, before the last light was out of the sky, but Shutok wanted to crawl away.

Hearing a flutter of wings, he looked up and saw the bird. It was on the hunters' rock, eyeing him, its head cocked to one side as if in doubt. His hesitation gone, Shutok whispered to himself, "Now!" He hoisted himself up on his crutch and stepped into the open.

They noticed him immediately. Shutok felt the strong, flat wind of their eyes upon him, forcing him either to bend into it or to step back. He stepped toward them.

His voice was thin at first, faint like the light that remained on the horizon, but singing was the language of Shutok's heart and his heart was full. The song swelled, high-pitched, wild, and disjointed. He watched the marsh people, stuck in their tracks, tense but curious. When he got to the level ground around the cave, Shutok cast aside his crutch and walked toward them on his own. At that the men murmured, not understanding what they were seeing. But the shaman knew. Shutok kept his eyes on him.

He stood taller than the others. Dirty red and yellow paint clung to his arms and face. He wore the birdskin robe, apparently the richest man among them, for the others wore next to nothing. Compared to their shaman, Shutok knew he looked very mighty indeed.

At Shutok's approach, the man's eyes revealed the true undersides of his thoughts like an aspen quaking in the wind, fear flashing white beneath his outward expression of scorn. When the shaman looked ready to run, Shutok raised his arm and pointed as if to fix him on the spot. The boy broke off his song abruptly and the shaman shifted his weight nervously from one leg to the other.

There was a dizzy moment when Shutok felt every one of his frustrations and humiliations rising inside of him and threatening to burst senselessly from his lips. He hesitated, not out of restraint, nor because the shaman spoke a different language, but because he did not know where to begin. That pause kept him from losing the mysterious dignity that was his only advantage over the shaman.

"What do you want with me?" the man signed. He had deferred, and Shutok knew he could have sent the man flying with only a gesture. But once again he hesitated.

The encounter was dreamlike and horrible. Shutok felt afloat in it, unable to touch down. There was something incomplete in what he was doing, something he had forgotten. He looked deeply into the shaman's face, as if he might see it there. The shaman raised his hand self-consciously, driving away the mosquitoes that were swarming everywhere. Shutok heard them buzzing. There were no other sounds. And then he remembered.

"Uita," he choked. "Come here." His voice had faltered at a critical moment and the boy struggled to hold himself. He did not want to have to use his voice again.

The girl stood beside him but he did not turn to look at her. He removed the skullcap so he could take one of the necklaces off over his head. To the shaman he signed, "For you, in exchange for the girl."

"No!" Uita protested. She caught Shutok's arm, forcing him to bring it back to his side.

"But you will be free!" he whispered. He felt as if he were hanging by his fingernails to a cliff after the ground had suddenly fallen away from under his feet. He looked into her face, his eyes pleading with her not to argue with him now. Then she left him standing there alone.

The shaman saw all of this and his manner changed. With his eyes he seemed to be saying to Shutok that he had not been able to fool him for long. His face was arrogant and sour — like the face of someone eating tainted meat, the boy thought.

Then in an instant Uita was back beside him. She gave something to the shaman. Shutok was hurt and confused. It was the necklace he had given her, the one Aar had taken from her earlier.

A voice behind him said, "Do you agree to this?" It was Aar. His voice had all the strength that Shutok's lacked.

"Yes," the boy answered meekly.

Aar stepped up next to him and signed to the shaman.

When the shaman nodded in agreement, Aar ordered, "Then go!" The shaman smiled knowingly, but he turned and led the others down the trail.

"Uita," Shutok whispered hoarsely. The last of the marsh people were watching, but the boy felt as if he were going to fall. "Help me."

15

SHUTOK'S FAMILY crowded around him, the women asking
questions, their eyes full of awe, the men dignified, silent,
but deferential. Coming so suddenly, the hunters' respect
made Shutok uncomfortable; no one stopped him when
he wanted to leave. Uita helped him down the trail and
across the creek to his camp, then stayed with him.

He ached everywhere — his back, the places Aar had
kicked him, his empty stomach, his head — but like the
skin a snake has shed, Shutok also felt empty and dry,
light enough to blow away in the breeze that ruffled his
hair. He lay down the way he was dressed and pulled the
bison robe over himself. Before he slept he said, "You gave
him the necklace, the one I made for you. He would have
taken one of the others."

Uita bowed her head beneath the hurt that sounded in
his voice and did not answer. The last thing he heard was
a lullaby, Uita's song, soft and warm and close.

In the morning he opened his eyes and asked, "Why?"

Uita sat beside the fire she had started sometime during
the night. Without looking at him she said, "Uita is no
one's slave. Not the shaman's, not Aar's, not Shutok's."

Shutok tried to speak, not knowing what to say, and choked on the words he could not find. He cleared his throat, looking up at the sky through a film of tears. Free! Uita was free, and to Shutok that meant two strong, brown legs gracefully parting the grass as he ran, a member of his band, a hunter. He envied the freedom that would let Uita be one of her own people again, for he could think of nothing that he desired more for himself. But it stung him to think that freedom for Uita meant release from him. Had it been that hard? he asked himself.

"How did you get the necklace back from Aar?" he said finally.

"I took it from him. After he saw you in the spotted pelt he knew I did not steal it."

The boy slept some more in the pause that followed, then woke with a groan. Uita was shaking him. "Wake up now," she said. "Yaiya, he's coming here."

Shutok's muscles were so stiff that he did not try to stand. His brother walked briskly through the brush, stooping once to duck beneath a branch without changing his step. He gave Uita a quick, appraising glance that Shutok did not like, then spoke.

"Are you all right?" There was concern in Yaiya's voice. He was asking this question on his own, not repeating it for someone else, and Shutok relaxed.

"Yes, but . . . I don't understand. We are not supposed to talk like this. You are a hunter. It is against the way."

"Aar told us all that you have a way of your own. Last night we sang victory songs because you helped us save face with our enemies. You and the girl are welcome in

153

our camp. That is what Aar told me to tell you. Are you sure you are not hurt?"

"It is nothing," Shutok said, looking away. He was suddenly bitter, remembering Yaiya's strong steps, the effortless way he walked.

"That's what you always say." Shutok looked up to see a smile on Yaiya's face. His own lips parted, then he threw his head back and they both laughed.

Yaiya cleared his throat, blustery and self-important again. "I will tell them that you are coming to eat with us then."

"Yes, we . . ." Shutok stopped, then corrected himself after shifting his eyes to Uita. "I will come in a short while," he said distractedly.

He waited until Yaiya was gone and then asked, "When will you be going?"

Uita shrugged, a vague look on her face, and Shutok wondered if she understood that freedom to go was also freedom to stay as long as she liked.

Then she let him know. "I am hungry," she said. "We will go eat now."